CLUB REVENGE

DYSFUNCTION AT ITS FINEST BOOK 1

J.M. DABNEY

HOSTILE WHISPERS PRESS, LLC

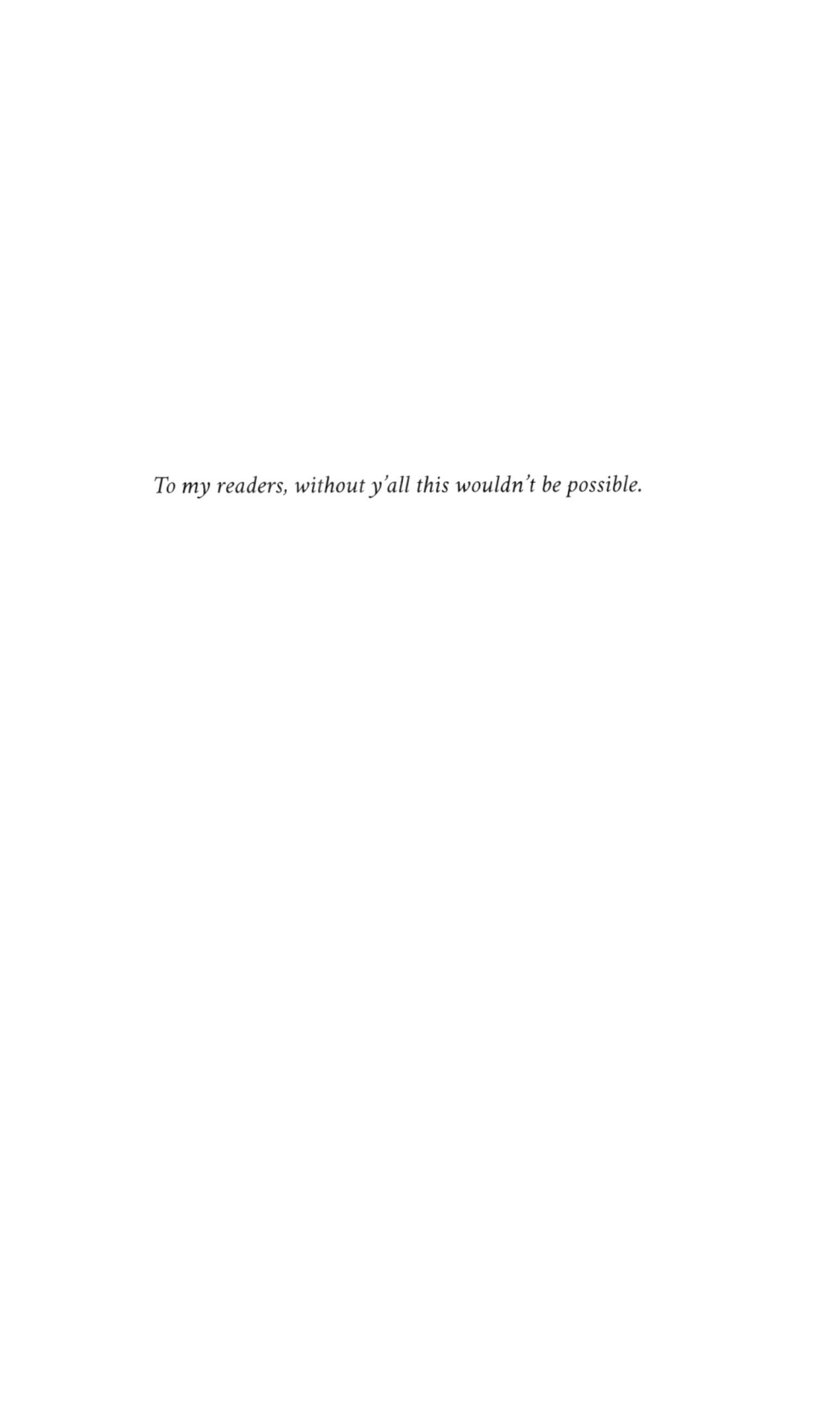

To my readers, without y'all this wouldn't be possible.

PROLOGUE

The screams are what awoke her, muscles once relaxed tensed at the sounds of her mother's pleas for mercy. Helena Medina-Jackyl never begged for anything. It was those pleas which had fear coursing through her veins. Helena was always the first at her husband's side in battle. They were warriors. Pure born vampires and one of the oldest bloodlines on record.

Her room was on the second floor directly above the study where her parents spent their early evenings. She stared up at the ceiling and focused on the muffled screams until they became clearer. Her father, Samuel, hissed and enraged, intensified by the blood-chilling scream that slipped passed her mother's lips. Throwing aside her covers, she rolled from her bed. Her bare feet silently crept over cold, wooden floors as instinct took over.

Trained for this moment, taught to ignore whatever screams she heard, whatever horrors she saw, her only task to save her siblings. Bram, a decade younger than she, he was first. She hugged the wall, blending into shadows as her fingers trembled. She grabbed the brass knob for his door, and she cringed slightly at the grind of metal-on-metal. She squeezed through the small crack between door and frame.

Bram's fingers circled her wrist, she met his fear-filled gaze, and still determination squared his slim shoulders. As the oldest, she'd learned to push away the fear, learned to control it, but no one told them of what would come after.

"Is it time, Amora?" Bram's voice wobbled on the verge of tears. She gave him a quick, comforting hug. It was the only comfort she could offer. When the night was through, nothing would ever be the same. The brave front was harder for Amora than she expected, and she could merely nod in answer.

"You must get the twins, take them to our secret place, and I promise I will come back for you. I swear that I will be back." Peeking around the edge of the door, left, right, and then she turned to give Bram the okay to go. To the casual observer, Bram's movements appeared to be no more than shadows shifting at the corner of her eye.

She didn't leave her post until Bram disappeared into Nicolette and Naomi's room. The twins never awakened until someone came for them. Seconds later, their cries for Mama and Papa brought tears to her eyes. She listened for the quiet murmurs of Bram consoling them, explaining as much as a child could. A child—she was one herself, but she had a warrior's job. Amora observed their progression out of the bedroom, and they headed toward the secret chamber where they'd wait for her return or that of their parents.

Her vision sharpened and she hissed quietly at the tiny, twin pricks of her fangs into her lower lip. The scent of blood floated in on the air. Amora made herself as small as possible. She stayed to the darkened edges of the hallways and followed the smell. Her palms connected with the floor, her back slightly bowed up as she scurried along the floorboards. She tilted her head back, and she scented the air. Her approach was silent as she reached the library where Mama and Papa spent their early evenings. Oil lamps dimly lit the room, pitiful whimpers, and loud curses echoed off the shelves, and she took in the scene.

Fear, rage, helplessness coursed through her as she saw Papa suspended with wooden spikes protruding from his shoulders. He cursed in an ancient tongue. Mama lay on the floor, curled into herself, and her arms wrapped around the swell of her abdomen. A crimson pool spread about her. As if Helena sensed her there amid her pain, she looked up and Helena's eyes filled with tears. Bloody drops flowed down Helena's cheeks. Amora was frozen there with fear. Helena mouthed the word, "Babies." Amora nodded, and her mama seemed to relax, as if she were giving in. Her split lips formed one word. "Run."

The scrape of metal against wood jerked her attention away from her mama. A tall, slender man swung an ax upward, the back of the blade cradled in his palm. He laughed, a sound filled with no mirth chilled her. He turned, and Amora took note of the black roses tattooed just visible above his collar. She felt her lips part as the ax came back in a high arc before moving through the air with just a whisper of sound.

A scream tore from her throat as the ax blade severed her father's head from his body. Her mama cried and crawled her way across the floor, and she surged to her feet. "Amora, run!" It was the last thing she heard as her mama lashed out with her elongated nails, flesh ripped, and the man bellowed in agony.

Figures in black clothing came for her. She turned and did what her mama bid her do, she ran. Amora escaped from the house and drew them from the estate house, away from Bram, Nicolette and Naomi. Tears scalded her cheeks.

Papa was dead. Mama and the baby still in her womb, would be as well. She couldn't save them, but she could save her siblings. Amora could give them a chance. Disappearance would have been easy, but she slowed her pace enough for them to keep up. She needed them behind her, to see her, and forget about the others.

She ran until muscles ached, miles passed in a blur of scenery and then she doubled back when Amora didn't hear them anymore. She hoped she'd lost them, and they had given up for now. The house came into view, ablaze—the babies, Bram. She picked up speed. She'd left them. It was her only task, to keep them safe. That was her job. Huge, thick muscled arms circled her out of nowhere, and she fought, clawed, bit, and hissed. Madness took over, desperation, and she fought, even as chains circled her wrists and ankles. They were all gone, she'd failed, and she'd lost them all.

I am Amora Medina-Jackyl, last of my Pure-Born Vampire bloodline, and vengeance will be mine.

CHAPTER 1

The deep bass pounded beneath the thick soles of Amora's boots. She crossed her arms over her chest and looked around Club Revenge with a sense of pride. She had been in New Orleans off and on for several years and walked the streets every night before she decided to settle in. Blues and jazz flowed from every open bar and club door. She'd lived countless places in her four hundred years of existence, but this one was the only one that called to the remaining vestiges of her soul.

Bodies moved on the dance floor, hands stroked overexposed, silky flesh or along corded muscle. Lust tinged the air, everyone in the room felt it and sensed the urgency. Any other night she would make her way onto the crowded dance floor to become lost in the sea of bodies. She'd find a warm body for the evening, draw the woman into her and get lost in the sensory overload—the scent of sweet skin devoid of the cloying stench of perfume, hear the breathlessness of her voice, and taste the salt of heat-dampened skin. *But not tonight.*

A few nights had passed since she had a perfect armful of female. Owning Revenge made it easy to find a lover for the night, but she grew weary. Her reputation, the thrill of lying with a monster, and they submitted easily. Sex was sex, too simple to get. Some lonely souls craved contact, unconcerned with the temporary nature—a well-cultivated cover for what they wanted. Amora shook her head and lifted her hand, whipped her towel from its perch and wiped down the shiny bar.

Last call approached, she signaled her performers, and they wandered from the direction of the stage and dressing room. Soon, Amora would lower the music and tell everyone it was time to go home, then she and her people would relax for the rest of the night. It was the only time she had a moment's peace because when dawn made its inevitable arrival, the nightmares—or more like day-mares— would come with the promise of strangling fear.

She tipped her driving cap lower over her eyes, then she went about setting up the customers at the bar with another round. Amora joked where it was appropriate, flirted with the women in hopes she'd find a distraction from what would come. Her lovers never stayed the day, she always ushered them out before dawn, her pride, or as some would say, arrogance wouldn't allow anyone to see the weakness of her fight against her demons. They were real ones, not just the ones who sprang from the bowels of a mythological Hell, but also flesh and blood ones. Witnesses to her every weakness—the blubbered pleas for her life, for sustenance. They'd starved her, and turned her into a weapon—*they* had stolen too many years.

Eighty-seven years locked in a cell, dying in small measures of time, her flesh became paper-thin. Gums receded, her body emaciated from the withholding of blood she had needed to survive. She learned the exact smell of her flesh as it burned—what it looked like falling as ash to the dirt floor. The horrors she had faced, the acts she had perpetrated haunted her, but she merely wanted to sleep, to find contentment and peace.

Her greatest regrets came to her in blaring clarity, all her mistakes, the faces of all the innocents, and the not so innocent, moved in a macabre play behind scratchy eyelids. Amora would feel the wetness of tears trailing down from the corners of her eyes as she fought each day to remain somewhat sane. Those tears were failures she wouldn't let anyone else see.

Amora always woke to screams and hisses, lingered pasts, realized the agony wasn't hers but that of her mother. She would curl upward, wrap her arms around her raised legs and rock, force the clinging memories away. Amora didn't know when or if she would find peace. With each year, decade and century that passed, her doubts of some happiness faded or shattered in the reality of her existence. All she had was an existence. She survived and little more than that. She found bliss in warm bodies, in the clasp of feminine legs and arms. An empty momentary sexual oblivion.

She shook off the thoughts. There would be plenty of time later. She immersed herself in her element, her comfort zone. Tasha, part-time bartender and full-time performer, set down at the bar, and Amora leaned across it. She braced her forearms on the surface as she kissed the silky warmth of Tasha's cheek. "Hello, Darlin'. What can I get ya?"

"My usual, please, Boss Lady. How did you fair with me on stage tonight?"

"Except for ya distracting me from my job shaking that sexy ass, I think I handled it just fine. You'd believe you 're the boss around here. Should I be concerned about my job?"

Tasha laughed, her ample breasts bounced in the tight confines of her tank top. "Not as long as you're signing my paycheck."

Amora smirked and pulled an icy, brown bottle from the cooler, twisted off the cap and set it in front of Tasha.

"Speaking of job, you're taking off to destinations unknown this weekend, right?"

"I have a little business to take care of. You know that, don't get nosy."

"Would I even dream of it?" The innocent flutter of Tasha's lashes didn't fool her—she'd known her too many years.

"Yes, yes you would." Amora quirked a brow as a greasy bruiser took the seat beside Tasha. She watched him as he was about to lean in. His massive, paw with its grease-encrusted nails grazed Tasha's bare shoulder. Amora snarled, her movements blurred as her slender fingers wrapped a crushing grip around the male's wrist. "In my establishment, we ask before we touch. Is that understood?" He fought the bruising force of her fingers. Amora leaned across the bar, bringing herself eye-to-eye with him, and she bared her fangs. "I wouldn't try it, fucker. You'll lose that fucking arm, and I'm sure it would put a damper on your sex life."

"Bitch, you better fucking take your hands off me, now." His eyes shifted from black to bright yellow.

The corner of Amora's mouth lifted higher as she moved in closer. "I don't know who you think you're fucking with, but ya keep pushing and it ain't going to end well for you. Move on." She released his wrist, and he reeled backward on the barstool. She coldly smiled as she straightened. Amora waited for him to make his move, advance or retreat. Either way, she was ready for him.

The bastard's chest expanded, his fists flexed as he debated his options. Amora's smile turned deadlier at his tells. It was a subtle twitch at the corner of his eye. Disappointment infused her chest as the shifter violently jerked away with a quick turn, and Amora shook her head. She was ready for a brutal battle forged in blood and pain. It was what she needed. A beautiful distraction, a feeding and a day of healing oblivion her reward for a victory agonizingly won.

"Do you do that on purpose?" Tasha asked.

"Do what?" Amora deflected.

"You damn well know what. Look for the biggest, craziest beast in the room to threaten?"

"Whatever do ya mean, darlin'? I was making a friendly suggestion."

"Uh huh, you were downright cuddly, Boss Lady."

Amora chuckled at the rolling of Tasha's eyes. "You got things handled around here for me?" She preferred to keep her other activities separate from Revenge and the less her employees knew, the safer they were. Especially her newest bounty, Amora wouldn't bring that kind of hell to her doorway.

Her latest mark wasn't the easiest to find. It had been three months and nothing but dead ends and rumors. She knew the vamp's reputation well, his history and his body count. His proclivity was for inflicting as much pain and suffering a body could take. They were monsters made of similar cloth, their only difference was she ended her victims' anguish. Boone liked to leave them with memories and scars to remember him. That couldn't be allowed.

"When haven't I handled everything? You do whatever it is you do, and I'll make sure this place keeps the booze flowing, and the girls don't stop shaking their asses."

"That's my girl. I'm going to take a walk, check the bathrooms and the shadows."

Tasha nodded at her and Amora walked from behind the bar. Her bouncers were reliable, but as with any male, they were led by their dicks—that wasn't just a *human* male trait. Faulting them for a warm body would make her a hypocrite. As the night waned, she prowled the edges of the room searching for the scent of lust and the irresistible lure of feminine arousal.

She'd existed so long to take revenge. Amora killed the ones who'd taken her parents, siblings, and her sanity, but it hadn't been enough. The hunt and the kill were what she knew. Were there more reasons to survive...no. There was too much blood on her hands and an endless index of sins. Retribution breathed down her neck, and the Devil wasn't known for his patience.

CHAPTER 2

*R*oad to Hell. The bar seemed aptly named situated in the middle of nowhere Texas near the Mexico border. She pulled her truck to a stop beside the long row of vehicles out front. Amora left most of her weapons behind except for the dagger holstered at the small of her back. She was merely there for information, yet trouble followed her wherever she went, so a weapon was necessary. An old ally waited inside, but she hadn't informed him she would be stopping. Hunters patrolled the area. Relics from a darker past ready to cleanse the Mortal realm of Preternatural abominations. The less they knew of her whereabouts, the better. Her own bounty was a temptation most wouldn't resist. Every night she thought it was a good day to die, yet her vampire ass wasn't ready just yet.

The door of her truck loudly creaked as she pushed it open and stepped out. Amora straightened to her full height. From beneath the brim of her cap, she cast her gaze from left to right and focused on the shadows for any sign of danger. Paranoia was second nature. She trudged toward the entrance. Amora paused at the door and prepared herself for whatever was on the other side. She flattened her palms to the rough-hewn surface of the door and pushed...

She cringed as she walked through the door. Loud music, thick smoke and the scents of stale sweat and beer assaulted her over-reactive senses. It was like slipping back in time. The wood planks of the floor creaked beneath her boots. Herder, an old friend from times long past and best forgotten, owned the hellhole. The bastard knew everything and his information was cheap—free if she played her cards right.

Amora pushed through the bodies dancing, well, more like banging on the floor. Herder's girls were as cheap as his information.

"Jackyl! Look what the Devil dragged in," the huge bear of a man said. She could see round, reddened cheeks and twinkling, green eyes above the bushy nest of a beard and beneath the well-worn cowboy hat. He hadn't changed much from the late 1800's when he had been robbing trains and banks.

"Herder, I see ya still own the same hat." Amora sat down on the stool in front of him, a shot glass and whiskey bottle appeared before she settled.

"It's my lucky hat, Jackyl. What brings ya to Road to Hell?"

"Looking for someone, no other reason to be here," she sardonically quipped. Talking bullshit was normally her modus operandi to ease her mark into revealing what she needed. If Amora laid on the charm, his suspicion would spike.

"I'm fucking insulted; this is a highly respectable establishment." Herder threw his arms out and motioned to the rotting shell of a bar.

She snorted and poured a drink. "Yeah, ya got some high-class pussy sashaying around here."

"If'n ya ain't here for the pussy, which I know you ain't, who ya looking for?"

She took the picture from her pocket and slid it across the bar. "Someone's keeping his ass in a safe house around here. I got some leads a few weeks back, and every one of them sent me this way. Besides, he likes ass and ain't particular. Any of your girls been doing house calls?"

"Not recently. A while back maybe a month ago, one of them, Adalaine, wanted to make a little extra cash. When she got back here, she was fucked up. I ain't never seen anything like it. We barely got her pieced back together, but she ain't said a word since she fell through those doors that night, won't even leave her room."

"What was the damage?" Before she twisted the cap back on the bottle, she slammed back a few shots and slid it across the bar.

Edgar Boone was a twisted fuck, mass murderer and sadist. She didn't know how he made it back topside and it wasn't her business. Amora only had to find him.

"We lost count of the stitches after the first couple hundred. Whatever he is, he's a biter, and he took some flesh to remember her by."

"Think I could talk to her?" Amora asked. It didn't matter his answer, she was going to speak with the girl and wanted to feel out what trouble awaited her.

"Ya can try, I ain't going to guarantee anything. Like I said, she ain't been real talkative. I could make it worth ya while if ya could find him and teach him a lesson or two."

"Surprised you didn't go after him yourself? Mellowing in your old age?"

"Naw, but a non-human can't be too careful, heard there's a few hunters around. They've been making their presence known recently. I like my head right where it is." He motioned toward the staircase and rickety banister. "Her rooms upstairs, fourth door on the right. Ya a real lady's woman so I am sure ya can handle the introductions. Just be gentle, Jackyl, the girl ain't exactly right anymore."

Ignoring his comment, Amora stood and headed for the steps. She made it quickly to the door. She lifted her hand and knocked, but didn't get an answer. What was she going to see on the other side? Amora had witnessed the aftermath of what Boone did before, read the case files and studied the photos of the mess left behind for others to clean up. She opened the door and stepped inside. Frightened eyes widened from a far corner, candlelight simmered off what she knew were tears.

Adalaine pulled into herself and watched her warily. The angry, red scar that ran from the corner of her lips to disappear into her greasy, tangled hair caused Amora to snarl. The room reeked of unwashed flesh and the decay of weeks' old blood. Amora reached up and removed her hat to throw it on the dresser to the right of the door.

"Adalaine, can I call you, Ada," Amora asked yet didn't wait for an answer. "I'm Amora. I want to talk to you about the bastard who did that, but if you're not ready to talk, I've got time." She hooked her fingers over the back of a wooden, straight-backed chair and carried it across the room.

Ada scrutinized Amora's every movement like a trapped animal. Whimpers muffled behind compressed lips. They were sounds Amora found all too familiar. They tore at the reins of control Amora held over the haunting memories. Setting the chair down, Amora straddled it and laid her arms along the top. Ada just continued to watch her, eyes narrowed, and her head tilted from side to side as Ada studied her. With all the visible skin stitched back together, the girl, no more than maybe early twenties, looked like a patchwork quilt.

"Don't worry, I'll stay right here and when you're ready to talk, just talk." Amora kept her voice soft and gentle, she hid her rage and ever-present thirst for vengeance. She'd felt the same when she hunted down the people who killed her family, the ones who had held her prisoner. Someone would pay for what they did, and she was the only one qualified.

Midnight drew nearer and still Ada remained silent, observed Amora from the corner of her uninjured eye, the other was barely more than a slit. Sudden movements and Ada moved deeper into the security of the small space between the wall and an armoire Ada lifted her arms as if to ward off a blow. Patience wasn't one of Amora's virtues, but at that moment, she was learning it the hard way. Amora's eyes took in every exposed inch of Ada. Although the scars would pale with time, years, decades, hell, maybe even a lifetime would pass, and she would remember the story brutally written into tender flesh.

She'd instantly sensed Ada as a kindred spirit, a survivor. She'd made eye contact with countless people, and all it took was looking into their eyes. It was a shift and change of emotions. Naked pain and then self-preservation took over, and gazes turned cold and steely.

Amora cleared her throat, Ada needed to start talking. The thin curtains weren't vamp friendly. "You remind me of myself. I was locked in a cell once, years inside stone walls. Starved until I was mad with it, would do anything just to feed and I did. Became a right good monster, a perfect little weapon, and I have almost as many scars as you're going to have. Do you know what I am?"

Ada barely shook her head, but her eyes told Amora she knew she wasn't human. She stood, worked the buttons of her shirt loose and laid it over the back of the chair. "A vampire. Not one of them turned kind—those are rare—I was born one, just as my parents and their parents before them. See this one right here?" Amora ran her fingertips over the uneven skin, the dips and hills of scarred tissue.

"They liked to throw open the curtains and watch me burn, oh, not to kill me, but they took pleasure in listening to me fight my screams. They severely starved me, and I never healed right. And these…" She crossed her arms over her chest, fingers pointed at the ridged skin. "Staked me to a wall through both my shoulders, took branding irons to me. I was too weak to fight. We survive. We keep going because sometimes we have no choice, darlin'."

Amora closed the distance and crouched down in front of her. Ada was tensed and trembling. "I may still be that monster they created beneath all these scars, but I would never inflict pain on someone who doesn't deserve it." Amora lifted her hand and gently traced the scar along Ada's cheek. It still bore the marks of poor stitching. Tears filled Ada's eyes, and Amora kept moving her hand until her fingers sank into the thick, greasy strands of her hair. They wrapped around the back of her head, and she tugged Ada to her. With her head on Amora's bare chest, the tortured creature fought with the last reserves of strength. Maybe her will to survive was gone. Amora gathered Ada onto her lap. Amora felt the warmth of tears against her chest. Ada's shoulders shook, and loud, painful sobs ceased only by her gasps for breath.

Time seemed to drag, a clock in the distance marked time with a quiet, predictable rhythm. Both of them locked within the sounds of grief, the stench of a sour body, but Amora let Ada cry until there was nothing left.

The sweetest sound came in the form of whispered words, a soft, girlish voice stuttered out horrors. Ada spoke, still locked inside and trapped by fear. Tales of torture bled out as the young woman's soul lay raw and bare. She talked about what he had done, relived each slice of his knife and how he made her watch as he skinned her side. Amora closed her eyes to hide rage in case Ada looked up, forced the feral growls to remain locked within her chest. She listened to words that became softer and quieter, faded in intensity, and breaths evened out as Ada fell asleep.

The exhaustion Ada fought finally won, and the young woman went limp in Amora's arms. Maybe for the first time in weeks, Ada felt safe enough to sleep. Ada's trust in the monster Amora was, humbled her. Amora would let her sleep for a little while.

Up until then, this had been a job, a paycheck, but now it was personal. No matter what she had to do, she'd find him.

CHAPTER 3

*T*oday was the day, Lark Banner fidgeted nervously and tried to stay on task. The musty odor of the old tomes that usually filled the library brought her comfort. It was her one bright spot in her life. Her appointment to Assistant Archivist made her invaluable, and she could speak and translate several languages. She didn't know why she could remember everything she read or studied. Most times it was a curse, but it kept her indispensable to Elder Falcon. He'd taken an interest in her from an early age due to her intelligence. No one else cared about her oddity.

Especially not since she was sixteen and the Elders of The Order of Angelus Kali relegated her to the role of Breeder. She was quickly running out of time and her twentieth birthday was only a few days away. Soon they'd give her to Reginald. He was the top Hunter of The Order—the one with the most recorded kills.

The Order would breed her, the sole purpose of her life would come down to how many children she could birth before her usefulness ran out. It sickened her, she had nightmares of being trapped beneath the brute as she did her duty to The Order. Law ordered assigned breeding pairs to produce as many children as possible. The only loophole existed when two Hunters mated—that word didn't seem right—they were to be battle ready at all times. She believed her parents only had Meadow to atone for the mistake of Lark's birth—to cement their status among the Hunters.

Her quickly approaching assignment pushed her to seek out a different life. She didn't crave the touch of a man. Her passivity made her an abomination in the eyes of The Order. Lark had hidden the secret since her first crush. She dreamed of what it would it be like—to find a woman to love as she wanted.

Lark dreaded what they would've done to her if they knew the truth. To deny tradition would make her life unbearable. Her parents had ceased acknowledging her existence years ago. Her one bright spot was her baby sister Meadow. Lark was heartbroken knowing she'd have to leave Meadow behind.

The plans made, it was difficult to hide money because they provided everything there. She'd barely put together enough to make her escape. Lark knew she needed to make it to America. She had a passport from the times she'd moved between a series of monasteries The Order used. They were rarely allowed outside the surrounding stone walls. Sometimes they took short trips to a nearby village for supplies. What was out there, terrified Lark, yet not as much as what would happen to her if she stayed.

To think back on the days when she thought they did good works ridding the world of monsters. Vampires, shifters, demons and the like, but her beliefs dramatically changed almost a year and a half prior. The Elders had them fooled, they didn't worship an angel or a God. Angelus turned out to be a vengeful demon who ordered the Elders to kill creatures whose only crimes were being a threat to the hierarchy. Centuries of death—mass murders—all perpetrated in the worship of a false idol.

They were nothing but a cult. Brainwashed by zealots who believed a quirk of genetics was an inferiority. Lark paid more attention to the comings and goings of the hunting parties, and the stories they shared on their returns. There were benefits to invisibility. She was weak and timid, naturally passive, in the eyes of The Order she was at the bottom of caste. No one left, dissension unheard of there and Lark didn't know or believe she'd survive her attempt.

She'd read the histories, heard the rumors and there was only one person who could help her. The Order imprisoned a Pure-Born Vampire for use as a weapon for nearly decades before she escaped and killed her captors. Amora Medina-Jackyl was synonymous with deadly. The list of her known victims in the archive astounded Lark, and she didn't believe the accuracy of the numbers.

The torture Amora withstood to survive, not to mention the fact she watched her entire family burn alive before The Order locked her away for training. Killing seemed all the vampire knew and Lark needed to find her. The rumors weren't enough, but if she could follow the tidbits of information she'd gathered maybe she could find a safe place to start. Stories circulated of a group in New Mexico who took in anyone if they asked for sanctuary. If anyone needed it, she did.

They'd scheduled a hunting party to leave at midnight, a supply vehicle would accompany them, and all she needed was to sneak into the van. It would get her passed the security points. At the first stop, Lark would exit the vehicle and disappear. At least that was the plan. Either way, she'd escape—death and freedom were the same.

* * *

THE RIDE WAS BUMPY, and bruises covered Lark body. She'd barely made it out. For some reason, twice the number of guards patrolled the compound. Certain they'd discovered her plan almost caused her to back out. She clutched her bag to her chest and closed her eyes. The proof of what The Order was really up to was inside her bag. The book held the evidence to prove her case for Amora's assistance.

Planning to face a killer wasn't her smartest move. If it were her only option of saving her sister, then she'd do what she had to do. The Order committed unspeakable atrocities upon Amora. She pulled all the details of what she read to the front of her mind. They'd chained the woman to a wall with shackles around her wrists and ankles and a collar that pushed spikes into the tender skin of her throat. The branding irons that burned crosses into her body. They would let the sun in to watch her flesh blacken and turn to ash.

The entries in the many journals spoke of her defiance and the captors that fell at her hands. What disturbed her the most were the stories of starving her until the powerful vampire was nothing more than a skeleton and crazed with thirst. At first, it was written Amora resisted the slaves thrown into her cell when her madness reached intensity for feeding. As with anything or anyone turned into a mind-less animal, she'd ceased the fight and took what she needed. The long-dead Elder's precise scrawl changed to an excited mashup of words when they'd successfully broken her—when they assumed they had broken Amora.

The night of the massacre, a survivor recorded Amora fought against her restraints until blood poured from her wrists and ankles. That the spikes penetrated fully into her throat. Amora didn't stop her struggles until the stone crumbled and she was free. She'd left bodies torn to pieces, drained of all blood, and the monastery burning. What kind of will to survive did the vampire possess to kill so many?

Lark shuddered at the thought. The sight of blood made her faint and nauseous. A Hunter she wasn't, and for the first time in her life, she regretted it. What struggles awaited her on her quest? Lark doubted she was strong enough to overtake them, but her sister's precious life was on the line. For Meadow, she would make a deal with the Devil herself.

CHAPTER 4

*A*mora only left Ada's side long enough to hunt down blankets to vamp-proof the room. She stood guard over Ada through the morning into the early afternoon. The need to sleep pulled at her as well, but she couldn't. Her nerves felt raw and exposed, a guarantee the nightmares would come. She paced the shadows, her fingers roughly tugged at her hair as she pushed them through her amber curls. She made herself stop the movements when Ada became agitated. Whimpers barely made it out before a scream pierced the still, musty air liberally laced with the scent of fear.

The petite, damaged body jumped from the bed, found the corner, and put her back to it. Ada's terrified gaze searched the room for danger and nails dug into peeling wallpaper. Amora quickly turned on every light, bulbs flickered then burned dimly. Each one that came on pushed the shadows back. Amora made a show of checking under the bed, inside closets and behind the shower curtain like a mother seeking imaginary monsters. Unfortunately, she, like Ada, knew not all monsters were figments of imagination.

"Do you remember me?" She kept her distance, shoved her hands into her pockets and rested her back to the door. The muscles in Ada's throat worked as she swallowed hard and then once more. Amora heard the angelic voice that belied the horror Ada had seen.

"Yes, y—you're Amora. Her—Herder tells us stories."

"Not good bedtime stories, I'm sure. You can come out of the corner, darlin', we need to have a talk." Ada slid up the wall until she stood, her fingers laced and she twisted them as she kept her eyes on the floor. Amora closed the distance, then she pulled her hands from inside her pockets and wrapped her arm around Ada. The top of Ada's head didn't reach Amora's shoulder. "You're a beautiful girl, but no one would know it under all that grease and grime. A body can't be healthy like that." Amora led Ada to the bathroom, the light was already on and she released Ada to turn on the rusted taps. Old pipes groaned while the water turned from a trickle to some semblance of water pressure. She put the stopper in the drain of the claw-foot tub and let it fill. "Strip on down, then get in, I'll be back in a minute."

She touched her back as Ada stood there stiffly. Amora left Ada to her privacy and walked to the bed, she removed everything from it. Amora gathered it all up to head for the door and held the bundle one-armed as she threw open the door.

"Lizzie!" One of Herder's girls waited as requested. "She's going to need new everything, and tell Herder, me and him are going have a talk about how he kept her." Violet eyes widened as she nodded her head with a jerk. She disappeared back into the room, picked up a ceramic bowl and an old tin cup and carried them to the bathroom.

Ada was in the tub, the water up to her pointed chin and Amora filled the basin with warm water. "Now, let's see what color your hair is." She placed the bowl on the floor and knelt. She wet Ada's hair and lathered the tangled mess. Ada remained silent, lost in her thoughts and she allowed Ada that time as she slowly washed weeks of grease and blood away. She brushed it to sleek dark, auburn curls. It reminded her of her mother's, only Helena's hair was an elegant silken fall around her shoulders. She had been elegant, a lady above all else, but hid a fierce, warrior beneath the proper breeding.

She finished her task, left the murky water there as she stood and closed the toilet lid to take a seat. "I was wrong." Amora smiled at the confusion on the too young face. "Not pretty, beautiful is more like it."

"No, no, I'm not. I'm a monster." Ada's fingertips danced over the scar on her cheek.

"No, I'm a monster. Boone, the bastard that I think did that..." She nodded to the scar. "Is a monster, but not you. Beauty is in surviving, learning to laugh and maybe even finding someone that appreciates you, scars and all."

"I can't pay ya for bein' nice to me, but I could..."

Amora growled at what the girl was about to offer and regretted it when Ada cowered. "We'll get this straight right fucking now; my kindness comes with no payment due. I'm not a whore, and neither are you." She held up her hand as Ada started to speak. "You may sell a piece of pussy here and there, but, darlin', you need to learn that your soul isn't for sale." Ada merely nodded and remained silent. "You stand under the shower and rinse. I'll get you clean sheets and some food. I meant it, circumstance doesn't dictate who we are, only we can do that. You can't change the past, but the future is up to you. We'll talk about that later."

At the soft knock on the door, Amora stood. She left Ada there, chin deep in water and tried to bring her anger under control. Ada didn't deserve it. Amora strode quickly across the room and opened the door to find the items she'd requested earlier. Quickly, she changed sheets. Set the food out and glanced toward the bathroom door.

When she looked at Ada, she saw a child in woman's form, someone that had never been given a chance. She would avenge Ada, get the girl her pound of flesh, and then she would make sure she always knew she had a choice.

She watched Ada long into the night as she slept, the walls closing in, hunger, the thirst gnawing at her gut. Amora turned away from Ada and headed downstairs for a little something to tide her over until she could have a proper feeding. Her gaze darted around the almost empty room and shot a look at Herder. He opened the cooler without a word, filled a rocks glass and set it before her. She didn't take the time to savor it, just downed the contents and returned to her new ward.

Dawn was a few hours away, and there were plans to make. Amora turned away from the sleeping form in the bed and made her way to the bathroom. She turned the rusty taps and quickly stripped. Amora pushed the curtain aside to step into the cracked, stained tub. She leaned her forehead to the broken tiles of the shower wall. Water cascaded over her head and back, the water like fire consuming the coolness of her skin. What the woman in the other room had gone through had ripped open festering wounds. Brought memories of the past forefront, ones that were once sweet and now, just tainted with horror and blood.

The action of trying to wash them away was at best, futile. She had scrubbed away layers of skin repeatedly only leaving bloody, raw flesh behind. Amora stayed in the shower as long as possible, she felt the approach of sunrise as an annoying ripple beneath her skin. She threw the plastic curtain aside, years of build-up made the once transparent curtain cloudy. Amora grabbed a towel and dried her skin roughly. Draping the threadbare towel over the back of the toilet, she finger-combed amber curls and dressed quickly in the jeans and a white, men's A-shirt she'd left on the bathroom sink earlier. Herder had sent one of the girls for Amora's bag. The fear she elicited was the only reason her things hadn't been picked through.

When she stepped back into the bedroom, she found Ada still asleep. Ada's body was deathly still and stiff. Even in slumber, Ada seemed on guard for any noise or sign of danger. She neared the bed, checked her one last time, and tucked the covers tighter around her. Ada was too young for this life. There was no hard edge to the girl. The attack had left Ada an open wound. Amora turned away from the bed, and she shoved bare feet into unlaced, black leather boots.

It was time Herder and Amora had a long talk about Ada's future. She closed the door and blocked out the sounds of the party still going on downstairs. Her heavy steps rang hollow on the old slat floors. She ignored the looks as she quickly descended the steps. Some eyes were suspicious, and others coveted what they stupidly thought they could have. Amora plopped down in front of Herder where he stood wiping down the grimy bar, and like the night before, he set the bottle and glass in front of her.

"I know that look, Jackyl, and it ain't boding well for me."

"Ada will be coming with me tonight, and that isn't up for discussion. This isn't the place for her and you know I'm right." Herder started to open his mouth, and she raised her hand to stop him. He was smarter than she thought when he closed his mouth with an audible click of his teeth. "I'm not listening. You let anybody at her, and I'm sure as fuck not going to let it happen anymore. I've got a safe place for her, and she'll learn to take care of herself without having to lie on her back for any fucker that pays you."

"I ain't that much of a bastard, Amora. It was her decision to hook up with that guy, and I ain't never forced her to stay here. She didn't have a place to go, and I gave her one."

"Great job. Now she's up there looking like a patchwork quilt. She should have had a backup when she went. You and I have been around long enough just to be able to look in a man's eyes and know he isn't right."

"That's un-fucking-fair! I watch their backs when they're here. I keep us under the radar. We don't make any waves, and we get left alone. Ya take that girl, ya do what ya can, but she was born to be a whore—"

The words barely left Herder's mouth before Amora's fingers were around his throat and she pulled him nose-to-nose. "You don't want to fuck with me, Herder, you know just what I'm capable of, and I will make your ass beg for death before I'm done with ya. I will skin you alive and keep a smile on my face while I'm doing it." He stumbled backward, his fists clenched at his sides, but he knew better than to fuck with her. She'd never made an idle threat. "We'll be leaving at sunset and there better be no trouble waiting for us."

Amora placed her palms flat to the bar, she stood up and her muscles clenched and rippled beneath her skin. She glanced over her shoulder at Herder's men. "Call them off, Herder, or you'll be looking for new muscle."

Herder didn't say a word, just nodded his head as she watched his Adam's apple bob with a hard swallow. She walked back upstairs and into Ada's room, closed the door and set the chair in front of it. Amora leaned it back onto two legs, her head rested against the scarred, wood surface and overlapped her arms across her chest. Sleep may come, but it would be light, Herder and Amora went way back, and she knew he wouldn't dare cross her. Although, she didn't have the same assurances about his employees.

She would take Ada to her old friend Seamus' camp in Osbourne, New Mexico, leave her in Fernando's care while she took care of Boone. Seamus was pack Alpha, the wolf and she didn't always see things eye-to-eye, but he was one of the few she trusted. Fernando was the Mother Hen of the pack and would instantly take Ada under his wing. The camp was the only safe place Amora knew where Ada would get the care and protection she needed. Her eyes closed and she drifted into the space between sleep and consciousness.

CHAPTER 5

$\mathcal{A}$da tried Amora's patience to the limit just to get her packed then out of her room. Amora tried her damnedest to understand, to remember what Ada had gone through and in some ways, still was. Ada lowered her chin and shielded her face from curious eyes. She carried Ada more than led her from Road to Hell. Ada seemed to understand why Amora was doing this, but that didn't cease Ada's bitching.

She'd contacted Fernando and explained the situation. As much as it pained her, Amora needed permission from the Alpha to add to his pack, even on a temporary basis. Seamus had agreed with more grace and mercy than she thought he possessed. They said they would put together a place for Ada to stay, but she told them not to worry. Ada could use her caravan. Amora wouldn't be there long. The only reason she was going to the camp was to get Ada settled and then it was back on the road. Boone couldn't run, not now. Having friends in extremely low places came in handy on occasion. She didn't know his exact location, but she knew the town. Promises of money for information was a siren's call.

Amora had enough of Ada's sulking, her pointed chin rested on her chest, and her eyes hadn't moved from her knees since they left

Road to Hell behind an hour ago. "You going to stay mad at me the rest of the way?"

"I...I coulda stayed with Herder." Ada sounded like a pouting child.

"Yes, you could've, but where would that have gotten you, huh? Do you want to be Lizzie? She used to have spirit once, but you can only get beaten down so much before you say enough is enough or break. I am not letting you break. Give the camp a few weeks. You don't like it, I'll get you back to your precious Herder. Deal?" She glanced at Ada and hid a smile at Ada's annoyed little sigh. With her small and delicate stature, Ada could be mistaken for a child.

She was amazed Ada had survived Boone's brutality. Physically, Ada's bruises faded, and the stitches removed from thick scars. Although mentally and emotionally, the nightmares would never go away. Scars would remind her with every glance in the mirror. Trying her best, Amora started to describe what the camp would be like—the people that would surround her. Ada seemed to understand, but the new and strange life would be alien to her.

Ada would be protected under Seamus' guard. Amora rolled down the window, she lit a cigarillo and lazily smoked as they rode in silence. The turn Amora needed to take was only a few miles ahead. When she reached it, smooth asphalt turned into a deeply rutted road, and Ada sat up straighter. The last five miles seemed to take longer than usual, wariness settled in about Ada's reaction. She pulled to a stop and cut the engine.

"Well, are you ready?"

Ada only nodded, and Amora opened her door, stepped out and scowled as a laughing Fernando appeared. He had an unconscious grace as if he moved like he danced to a silent tune. Slim fitted pants rode low on his hips, and his upper body was bare. She still saw him as the mangy half-dead pup she'd rescued years before and he thought he was Goddess' gift to man or woman.

"Amora, you know what happens when you don't feed. Drink, you look like shit." She glared as she took the wineglass, lifted it to her mouth and sipped the warm blood.

"It's so great to see you too, Fernando," Amora set the glass aside.

"Now, meet Ada, she's going to be your new best friend." Maybe it wasn't fair to sic the shifter on Ada, but they were going to be attached at the hip until Amora hunted down Boone. Ada might as well get used to the annoying shifter now.

"Oh, she's tiny. We'll have to feed her. Come, come, I don't have all night." Fernando threw open Ada's door and dragged her out. "Seamus wants to see you, Amora, don't keep him waiting." He led Ada to the fire. Amora sneered as she listened to Fernando ramble on and she headed in the opposite direction toward the Alpha's tent.

A guard she recognized greeted her with a tip of his head. He swept the flaps of the entrance to the side.

"Amora, I'm so glad to see you again. Please, come in, we've been waiting for you." Amora walked into the sprawling interior, pillows and rugs covered the center, and Seamus lounged with Yvette in his arms.

"Jackyl, where is our newest member of the family?" Seamus was a big bear of a man. Barrel-chested and powerful, he gave off an aura of danger even stroking the curve of his wife's belly.

"She's with Fernando. I appreciate this, Seamus."

"No matter what's happened, we've always been allies and friends when the time is needed. Are you going after her attacker?" Seamus asked. Yet, Amora knew he already had the answer.

"There's a bounty on him, I have to finish the job. But after what he did to Ada, it's more than that now."

"I understand that, Amora, and I even agree, but do you need to do it alone?"

Seamus' question didn't surprise her. He'd tried to get her to take back up when she'd gone on the initial search weeks ago. She'd run into several brick walls in her quest. Although Amora was certain she'd found him this time.

"Again, I appreciate the offer, no one else needs to be involved. If I need to, I'll call you to send me a few men."

"Fair enough, Amora, and when you come back, I expect you to stay for a while. Take some time to heal. You can only run from your demons so long before they catch up with you. Go, drink, rest and tomorrow you can seek your revenge for the girl's honor."

Without hesitation, she escaped before the words were out of his mouth. Amora stepped out into the chilly night. It had been days since she'd fed and a single glass wasn't enough. She ducked into the darkness and kept her distance. Music, laughter, and the crackling of numerous fires came from every direction. The scents of dinner and blood wafted on the gentle breeze. Once again, she was on the edge, alone within a crowd, and it was even more apparent in the tight-knit camp.

Was she supposed to belong there? She liked shadows and silence, but Yvette was determined to drag her into the fold.

Was there some light waiting for me?

Amora would make her excuses as she always did when Seamus tried to convince her to stay. Club Revenge and just one more job always were the first reasons out of her mouth. She just needed to find a purpose to quit running. But was that possible?

Amora strode back into the crowd in search of a meal. Dozens of hands moved over her, male and female, silent pleas for attention as bodies undulated against hers. The aroma of desire, wood smoke, and sex thickened the air. She snagged a glass of blood, lifted it to her nose and inhaled the richness. Amora exited the Mess tent.

Couples and groups drew together in writhing masses. The hairs on the back of her neck rose as she spun in the crowd of human and non-humans alike. She searched, her fingers flexed and fragile glass shattered. Shards glittered in firelight like hundreds of stars. Danger or curiosity, whatever it may be, her defenses took over, and she charged out of the crowd.

Amora's visions focused, all senses on alert and she automatically reached for her weapon. The sheath was missing from its regular spot at the small of her back. She was supposedly among friends and allies, yet her fangs still dropped. Her monster resumed control, and she darted into the darkened spaces between brightly painted caravans.

Fear, the alluring scent more beautiful than the most expensive perfume. Her steps were whisper-soft as she moved among the trees.

Confusion filtered into her hunger-fevered mind as something else accentuated the fear. Amora focused on the scent she hungered for and growled as it became stronger. A flicker of movement, a billowing of a skirt as quickened steps turned into pounding as her prey ran.

The predator rippled beneath her skin, and she lost herself in the hunt. The snap of fabric and stumbled steps alerted her to her prey's path, and she darted to the right. With ease, she could overtake the female, but the anticipation made the victory sweeter. She laughed cruelly as she caught up to her quarry, she reached out, and her fingers dug into a soft upper arm. Amora spun her prey as they fell to the ground. Her human prey was defenseless and fragile. Huge, almond shaped eyes stared at her. The exact shade obscured by darkness and panic with the pupils blown.

Her prey's terror was like the strongest of aphrodisiacs, Amora nuzzled the rose petal softness of her throat, and the pulse fluttered wildly beneath the tender flesh. The prey's curved body trembled beneath her. Amora's prey fought and clawed, oh, how she loved the fight before she took what she needed. Others of her kind may charm the mind, make the prey complacent, but that would lessen her terror, and that was what Amora craved the most. The adrenaline-laced thickness flowed sweetly over her tongue as Amora licked over the woman's lips.

Years had passed since she'd tasted the bounty of a hunt. The thrill of the chase, she lowered her head, again her lips barely brushed skin, and her meal flinched. The corners of her mouth tilted and stretched. She inhaled deeply of musky flesh and darted her tongue out to taste the saltiness of skin. Amora dragged the tips of her fangs along her prey's throat causing the female to freeze in her arms and braced for the pain of the bite. The only thought was of the resistance of flesh she knew would give sweetly under the pressure of her teeth. The woman knew fighting would do no good, knew the beast was stronger and intent on having what she needed.

Blood, it was a junkie's fix, like heroin or coke, she was lost in her body's need to feed, to survive. She could strike, take in the span of a blink, but there would be no satisfaction. The longer she drew it out, the better it would be. Oh, it would be so perfect. Amora's long fingers slipped into her hair, twisted the strands with slow, deliberate motions and Amora moaned at the resistance. She darted her tongue out to taste the first precious drops. Amora closed her eyes, prepared to savor it just as claw-tipped fingers knotted in her hair and yanked her head back.

Amora hissed as she surged to a crouched position. The thirst was a madness that imprisoned her control. Seamus crouched low. Black fur covered his bunched muscles as he reached the cusp of his shift.

"Amora!" His voice was a great roar that trembled along the ground, his body uncoiled, and he leaped forward. The force of his body tackled her and threw her off balance. Amora countered with a push, and she threw him back. Howls and hisses broke through the peaceful night as yelling joined orders for help. Strong arms twined around her from behind and spun her until she lay face down. She spun and her elbow connected with Fernando's jaw. He snarled, and more weight joined his—a great mass of bodies piled atop hers.

Voices called her name, anger covered the scents of fear, and she felt the retraction of her fangs. She gazed up into concerned black eyes. "You back with us, Amora?" Fernando asked.

The crawling beneath her skin increased, and pain ripped through her abdomen. She hissed as she banged her head back onto the ground and sunk her elongated nails into the tender hollows of her palms.

"Fernando, I've got her. Take Lark back to camp. Amora and I need to have a talk." The anger in Seamus' single grunt slipped into her consciousness as the predator faded out. She turned her head and noticed the young woman, Lark, curled beneath Fernando's protective arm.

Amora didn't want to talk. She wanted searing pain and exertion. She needed the fight Fernando interrupted, but more than that she needed the taste they had robbed of her. The predator stalked in the dark corner of her mind, and it would have what it wanted. Amora dug her nails in deeper, the split skin stung and sent a shiver through her. She pushed the monster a little farther back. For now.

"Amora," Seamus roared her name.

She forced her gaze from the slumped feminine figure. Amora suppressed the compulsion to demand her friend release the woman —to bring her back. From her supine position, she vaulted easily to her feet and lowered herself into a crouch position. The need to fight warred with her respect for Seamus.

"You can't keep on like this, Amora. She's nothing more than a child." The sadness and disappointment in Seamus' tone made her regret her actions—almost.

"I don't need your fucking lectures."

"Too damn bad, you're getting one. I won't allow you to hunt my people. What would you have done if we didn't get here in time?" Seamus asked.

"Fed," Amora answered with brutal honesty. A hidden part of her, one she'd long buried, urged her to feel something other than blood-lust—desire.

"We've been friends and allies for over a century, and I've allowed —" Amora advanced, cutting off what Seamus would say next.

"Allowed? You've let me do nothing," she hissed.

"Shut up, Jackyl, you're not a monster, you're more than what they created in that goddamn cell. I won't countenance your self-destruc-tion anymore. Over the last three centuries, you've done everything to live down to your training. Will you attack my mate if the thirst gets to be too much one day?"

"I would never touch Yvette," she bellowed and clenched her fists.

"How can I be sure of that? You chased down an innocent and attacked her."

"It's none of your business." The beautiful stranger, Lark, her scent still overwhelmed Amora's senses. It wasn't the usual craving—the need to only feed and fuck—this had been something different. What it was terrified her more than the nightmares or the threat of captivity.

"Don't make me have to kill you, my friend, the battle may be bloody and more than likely I wouldn't win. But you pull this shit again, I'll put you down. Don't push me, Amora." Seamus turned away.

"Someone will keep an eye on you until you leave. You're a danger to my pack members, and I never thought I'd ever say that."

The threat and promise in Seamus' voice were clear. He wouldn't hesitate to end her life. She could've forced his hand and dragged him into a fight. Dying in battle was an honor, Valkyries swooped down to take those who'd earned an honorable death and their place in Heaven —Valhalla. It wasn't for Amora, there wasn't anything noble in her battles. Maybe her intentions skirted the edges, but in the end, all she wanted was her fix. The sweet promise of fear and the rush of her one real high.

Amora straightened and watched one of her oldest friends walk away from her. Seamus disappeared into the line of trees. She instantly sensed a wolf and leopard in the darkness. Seamus could have his power-play and treat her like a wild animal because Amora was just that. She was only instinct. The desire to survive by any means necessary.

Although, one of the last remaining pieces of her humanity cracked. Amora was a monster, no more than fangs and cruelty. She shook her head and retreated into the shadows in the opposite direction from the camp. The truth was, she couldn't be trusted, and sooner or later she'd meet her demise. Because as Seamus believed, Amora was a dangerous animal in need of death. She just wasn't ready to die today, maybe tomorrow.

CHAPTER 6

*H*er chest hurt from the painful pounding of residual fear that coursed through her veins. Lark made herself as small as possible beneath the lean strength of Fernando's arm. She curled her fingers into his shirt and dared a backward glance. The woman and Seamus half-shifted form faced off. All fang and claws, foreboding energy filled the clearing. She must have paused because Fernando gently tugged her along.

"Nothing worth seeing there. Leave them to work out who's the biggest, bad ass Alpha."

"What will happen to her?"

"Amora will be all right."

"Amora, that's Amora Jackyl?"

"All six-foot-plus of fang and bloodlust. What do you know about her?" Something in the way he asked the question caused her to stiffen. She answered with a partial truth.

"Rumors," Lark blurted out. Suddenly the memory of someone, Seamus maybe, calling the vampire by Amora. That was whom she came for? Lark reached for her throat and traced the tender scratches formed by deadly incisors. She couldn't put her sister's life in the hands of that—Lark stopped herself from completing the thought. The people she'd escaped from months before were the ones who made Amora the way she was. Still, she couldn't allow Meadow into Amora's custody.

She tripped over an exposed root of one of the oak trees surrounding them. Fernando steadied her. She was hyper-aware of the nocturnal sounds of animals scurrying about in the brush. She wasn't sure if the flapping of wings above were from a bat, owl, or a shifter in their animal form. Aware of the faint scent of wood fires. It was strange yet familiar, the uncertainty of her place on the food chain frightened her. At least with The Order Lark knew where she stood—expendable. Not one of the people in her life, especially her parents, would've stepped between her and a creature such as Amora.

"Hold on, we'll be back at camp soon. I'll take you to see Yvette."

Why would Fernando take her to see the Alpha-mate? Would they order her to leave? "Have I done something wrong?"

"Of course not. Yvette is going to advise you to demand restitution for Amora's attack. When Seamus returns, he'll ask what your decision is."

"Restitution?"

"Pack members can demand punishment for violation of our laws. Amora attacked you, so you've got the say in what happens to her."

"I don't want that. Isn't it just natural in relation to predator and prey?"

"We're not animals, Lark, we're humans with animal halves or spirits. Vampires aren't mindless killing machines. Preternatural doesn't mean unnatural."

"But doesn't instinct play a part?"

"You're just full of questions, maybe talking with Yvette and Seamus would be of more help."

Fernando's icy tone ceased further interrogation. They stepped out of the trees and into a dimly lit circle of lanterns that enclosed the perimeter of the camp. Fernando led her straight down a path to a large brightly colored tent abutted to an equally sized rock formation.

The Alpha's caravan situated close to it. She stepped away from Fernando and hugged her middle. Guards swept aside fabric from the entrance.

"I'll leave you here. Amora entrusted me with her latest project. I've got to make sure it's behaving better than her."

Lark nodded in answer and entered the tent.

"I've been informed you've had a bit of excitement tonight." Yvette's petite frame backlit by a cozy fire in a squat, pot-bellied stove.

"Being hunted is a new one for me."

Yvette's lyrical laugh eased some of Lark's tension. "Amora makes life interesting around here, but usually our old friend is much better behaved."

"For some reason, I doubt that."

"Okay, I'll admit she's a bit much. Please come and sit so I can take a look at your throat." Yvette motioned to thick cushions around a low dining table.

"I'm fine, it's nothing but a few scratches." She didn't want to talk, yet out of respect, she took a seat.

"Our Amora isn't one to leave just scratches. If Seamus hadn't intervened, there'd be a funeral in the morning."

"What does restitution mean?"

"Amora committed a crime against you when she attacked without provocation. You can demand punishment."

"I don't want her punished."

"Lark, our laws are in place for a reason. The Preternatural Council is extremely clear about its members abiding by the rule of humans remaining ignorant of all the supernatural species. Amora knows better than to expose herself to humans."

"But you're human."

"Hence our pack's outcast status. We're a bit of an abomination but we stay to ourselves and secrecy is a priority. Most of the ones who came to us already knew."

"Why are you outcasts?"

"Preternatural species exist in the shadows. It's the way of the beast...the way it has been for millennia. Some believe breeding with humans weakens the bloodline." Yvette's hands stroked over the curve of her belly. "I panicked a bit when I realized I was expecting the first time and I ran, I swore I'd bring shame to Seamus."

"How many children do you have?" Yvette's features softened.

"We have five, six with this one. Our oldest is already a grown man, he turned twenty-five a few months ago."

Yvette didn't look old enough to have a son that age. She was curious, "Did Seamus turned you?"

"No, that's all movie sensationalism. Most are born, but sometimes there are anomalies. Mutations mostly in species that are unable to breed."

It was too much information. She'd studied her books and all the records, but there seemed a lot she still didn't know. "I don't want Amora punished."

"I don't either, I understand Amora and have known her for a long time. She and Seamus have a tumultuous relationship, but always in each other's corners. Although, they have drawn blood in a lot of battles between the two of them. Now, are you okay?"

"As okay as I can be after being hunted by a vampire."

"I guess I can understand that. Why don't you get a drink and rest? I'll relay your wishes to my mate."

"Thank you, Yvette. I do appreciate being allowed to stay here."

"You're welcome here as long as you need."

Lark stood and strode toward the door. She needed some time alone. Everything she'd learned and seen since she'd slipped from The Order's van when they'd stopped for gas overwhelmed her. The fact of being hunted by the very person—no vampire—she'd searched for the last six months was the final straw. She was exhausted and unable to figure out her next step. In her naivety, she'd expected something different. No, she didn't think getting Amora to help would be easy, but razor-sharp fangs at her throat weren't in the scenario.

She avoided the rest of the camp and rushed back to the caravan they'd assigned her. It was time to change strategies. She didn't know what that would be though. Lark darted a glance back toward the direction Fernando led her from earlier. She ascended the three steps while she searched for some sign of Amora. Violent vampire or not, she still needed the woman and hoped Seamus hadn't gotten rid of her last option.

CHAPTER 7

The night was too quiet, she tried to focus on the mission at hand, but the previous evening repeatedly played in her mind. Seamus threatened her, Yvette's quiet concern, and through it all, the hunger still raged. Even after the killer subsided and left her on edge, the thirst still lingered. Flashes of the woman, her scent, the wide-eyed stare and the acquiescence to her fate, yet she had fought. The truth was a bitter reminder, could the sweet stories her mother and father told her of love be right—of one made just for her?

She wanted to deny it and fight the inevitability of it. At one time, back before the hell of her cell she'd believed, yet no longer. A mate— she mentally snarled at the word—didn't exist for Amora. Her fingers curled and tightened around the steering wheel, she didn't have time for a distraction. Amora had a job to do, and any thoughts beyond what awaited her made her job more dangerous. Therefore, she concentrated on the present and left the rest for later.

Amora sat in her pickup that was more rust colored than dull, black paint. She'd left before the sun had barely set. Seamus and Yvette already tried to talk her out of doing what she needed to do. Leaving her guns behind was a big mistake to them, but knives were quieter and less likely to draw attention. Boone surrounded himself with humans, weak-willed automatons who would do his bidding without question. The only challenge was the shifters who patrolled the grounds of the small compound. They moved about scenting the air, and she observed them, the five sentries appeared as weak-willed and incompetent as the rest.

She didn't mind a battle. To be honest, she craved the bloodshed that Seamus robbed her of the night before by his interference. Tonight no one would stop her, she welcomed the imminent pain and the possibility of an end. She accepted the possibility of her death, and it made it somehow easier to walk into the uncertainty of her eternity. Amora couldn't care what happened beyond that moment. There were no guarantees she would be alive-ish when the sun rose. Amora pulled the door handle and stepped down, then she removed the black leather jacket and cap. The weight of her knives were heavy against her ribs, the sheaths secured by the leather straps over both shoulders, and she bent and slipped the dagger from her left boot.

She savored the familiar feel of the hilt and flipped the knife to lie along her skin. The steel edge was cool along her forearm. She silently stepped along uneven ground, her pace unhurried, and although it may be a good night to die, Amora still wasn't fucking ready. The scents on the breeze were of unwashed bodies and decomposing corpses, whether that was human or animal, she didn't care. Amora stopped, her long, slender fingers wrapped around the iron bars of the fence. It was only a foot taller than her six-foot-one. She bent her knees, pushed upward easily jumped the fence and crouched down. Her eyes scanned the darkness.

The howling took her by surprise for only a moment and then quickened her steps. A huge shadow illuminated from behind by the pale moonlight appeared in her path. She watched the beast with narrowed eyes as the dance began of opponents measuring their prey. The behemoth's eyes flashed, and a cocky smile curved his lips. The first rule of battle was never to underestimate your opponent. He lunged toward her, and he was about to break it.

Razor-sharp claws grazed her side as she spun to the right. Amora brought her arm upward, the steel of her blade sliced and bisected the valley of his spine. He roared in pain, pivoted on clawed feet, and the scent of blood infused the air. Amora's fangs pricked the inside of her lip, and her thirst intensified.

Their dance continued, each drew blood in turn until claws grazed Amora's cheek. The skin split, with searing pain, she hissed loudly, and she swung her arm. Amora brought the knife around with an arc and blood sprayed across her chest and face as his throat opened in a gruesome smile. His eyes were wide in horror, his hands gripped his throat with futility, and the blood flowed in a crimson fall down his torso. His knees hit the ground as he fell forward. She quickly straddled his back, gripped his hair in one fist and severed his head the rest of the way. Amora stood, the weight of the bastard's head bumping against her thigh and she calmly walked toward the house.

Amora tried to anticipate where the others were. By earlier count, there were four left. The thunder of feet alerted her seconds before they surrounded her on all four sides. She turned in a slow circle, they growled and lunged forward. They tried to make her flinch and show weakness, but that wasn't an option. Amora wouldn't break, and if she were meant to die, she'd go out fighting. She threw the head upon the ground in front of the biggest of the four. Her gaze coldly challenged him and calmly removed the second knife from its sheath. She flipped it to mirror the one in her other hand. Amora lifted her hands and waited for all hell to break loose.

The wait wasn't long as they attacked from all sides. Amora met them strike for strike, blow for blow, and for every drop of blood they drew, she drew more. The pain sent a rolling shiver beneath her skin, and she struck, the blade with a momentary resistance pierced the vulnerable underside of his muzzle. Two down, three more to go.

The fight could have lasted for minutes or hours, but each one slowly fell. The night air-dried the blood upon her skin and hair. Amora straightened to look down at the bodies at her feet. She stepped over them, and she continued to the house sheathing her weapons as she went.

There was nothing now, no fear or mercy. The monster from the cell was in complete control, and it pushed at the bounds of what sanity she had scraped together. Amora's strides were sure as she ascended steps and kicked the front door. The wood splintered, and Amora entered the brightly lit foyer. She smiled coldly covered in blood, and she could only imagine what she looked like. Her gaze cast from left to right and then left again.

The atmosphere was thick with fear—a tangible entity in the house, hearts pounded and pushed terror-laced blood through the veins of the occupants. Her tongue circled the sharp tip of her fang as her mind cleared of all but how sweet it would taste. Amora tilted her head from side to side searching for the loudest and fastest beat. She picked it out, her skin felt too tight and hunger gnawed at her gut. Amora went in search of what she needed.

A small slip of a man darted out of sight, and she changed direction in pursuit. She enjoyed the scurried whispers of his feet as he tried to flee, and then the sound ceased. Amora rounded a corner, she reached out and grabbed thin hair that barely covered the skin of his scalp. He yelped and cowered, she threw him away as she felt a presence behind her. Amora deftly twisted on her toes and struck before the coward behind her had a chance.

Amora hissed, her hand wrapped around a man's throat and she met eyes nearly as cold as hers. There was something crazed that stared back at her. Maybe hers looked the same. Amora pivoted once again on her toes and slammed him back against the wall. She heard the give of drywall and the rattle of frames. Her senses came back to her as she steeled herself for another battle and when she spoke, her voice was low and husky. "Boone." Her tone was deadly with no warmth.

"Medina-Jackyl, we finally meet in person. Are you to be my executioner?" His voice mocked her as he tried to make Amora lose control and strike out in anger.

"I was thinking about it, but we got some business to discuss first." Amora removed one of the knives from the sheath, she lifted it to drag the sharp edge across his cheek exactly where Ada's face bore his mark. "I hear you like to play the big bad man, leave a woman with a few scars to remember you. To make it fair, I thought I would return the favor, as I'm more equipped than she is. Do you even remember her name?"

Boone was a slight man, slender and unassuming, and it had always been his out. No one would expect that a fiend lived inside the mediocre shell. An animal who could walk through a room unnoticed, yet she'd seen firsthand what he was capable of, and that was before she ever set eyes on Ada. Amora's fingers constricted around his throat, she turned and she thrusted him toward a nearby chair.

"She was a whore, they're all whores, and these humans are nothing more than cattle, here for us to feed upon. You've done your share of killing. I've heard the stories of the bodies left in your wake."

"I fed, hunted to survive—" The lie fell too easily from her lips. "And I took great pleasure in the kill, but it was a kill, I didn't leave any alive. Ada deserved protection, I expected better of Herder than to let you live. She's barely more than a child." Amora ignored the echo of Seamus' statement in her head. As much as she wanted to let all the anger out, she couldn't and pushed aside the memories of the woman from last night. She tensed as she realized what she was doing and ignored the siren's call of her scent that still lingered in her memory.

The coldness of his laugh cut through her like a frigid wind. "She was no child, she knew what was going to happen. I was going to use her body as I saw fit and I did, repeatedly, all the while she begged me to stop. Her whimpers were *beautiful*. Maybe I should find her again, even for a whore she was so...innocent."

"No, Boone, you won't be getting near her or anyone else ever again, but we have a few things to take care of first." Amora leaned in and inhaled. "Let's begin."

"Do your worst. You won't break me and pretending this is retribution won't make you less of a killer, Jackyl." His words didn't take away from the building terror she sensed.

"You're right," Amora easily agreed.

Pale flesh split open as the deadly sharp blade effortlessly sliced skin. First, she opened his cheek into a gaping wound, the skin peeled back from his teeth and jaw. Amora placed one hand on his chest and held him in the chair. He sat there, a stony façade in place, but fear blossomed in his eyes. His precious blood slowly seeped from his body, his skin going from naturally pale to ashen and she continued. Boone refused to give in, she almost admired his courage that bordered on stupidity. Amora stroked her hand upward and enclosed his throat in an iron grip.

She picked the buttons from his shirt one by one with the tip of her blade. While she'd tended Ada, she'd memorized every scar with the intention of giving them all back to Boone, but Amora wasn't just here for the kill, she wanted him to suffer. Each cut deeper, she coldly sneered as his stoic shell broke. Boone's nails clawed at her forearm, and he kicked at her legs. She ignored the minute injuries as they were nothing compared to what she'd already experienced. He whimpered and began to beg, and those pleas fell on deaf ears. "Are those whimpers and pleas for mercy sweet now that they are falling from your lips?" He gurgled as the wound on his cheek caused his blood to flow down his throat.

Amora continued until not an inch of his flesh didn't bear marks that seeped crimson, Boone was too drained to fight back. Ada's scar-ravaged body played on repeat in her memories.

Everyone had fled, and the house was quiet except for Boone's labored breathing and pain-filled groans. Amora released him, straightened, and slipped the knife back into its sheath. She leaned forward, easily threw his form over her shoulder and carried him outside. She tossed him to the ground and left him there.

In the madness that tinged her mind, there was a terrifying sense of calm. The peace she found in the retribution for the innocent maybe one day she'd shed enough blood of evil beings to even out her slate.

She arrived at her truck, grabbed the bag from the truck bed and carried it back to where Boone stiffly lay. The rasp of the zipper loud in the quiet night. She quickly drove four stakes into the ground and pulled out the specially charmed rope for this job alone. "I can assure you this won't be pleasant. If I were you, I'd start praying for death right about now."

Amora spread him out, secured the ropes, and tested them until satisfied that they wouldn't give as he fought. "Do you have anything to say? More pleas for me to spare your life?" She placed her feet on either side of his hips and leaned down, his words were nothing more than whispers, broken words spoken incoherently. "I've been through this before, the searing pain and your flesh becoming ash. The scent of your skin burning is something that never quite goes away." She cringed as the words brought back the memory. "I still remember it like it was yesterday. Letting you die and not repeating this experience over is the only kindness I'll give you."

She stretched to her full height and tipped her head to gaze up at the sky. The sunrise approached, and there was enough time to reach the motel. It would act as her safe house where she'd sleep the day away. Boone tugged at his restraints. The rage in his gaze promised an act of payback he wouldn't survive to enact. Amora turned and strode away. She never once looked back, not even while Boone begged, and called her back.

Ada would sleep at night without thoughts of a monster that would stalk her from the shows. Vengeance had been done. But would it be enough? It was just another name on the long list of her victims. Amora's kills amounted to staggering numbers. What was one more added to the thousands already awaiting her day of judgment?

CHAPTER 8

*I*t wasn't as it should be, the dream, no, it was different than the nightmares before. This wasn't visions of a cell with one window dressed by a tattered and almost translucent curtain of floral print. No soft breeze of fresh air pushed away the staleness of the cramped space. There was nothing to at least let her see a glimpse of the outside world. Amora forgot how much she missed those dancing slivers of moonlight on gray stone walls or blood-soaked dirt. Panic made her pale skin damp with sweat, she extended her arms until her palms met wet, rough-hewn wooden slats.

Amora locked within some box or coffin. Fear took her throat in a choke-hold, and long, broken nails clawed at the walls of her prison. Her vision adjusted to the darkness. The putrid, stench of decayed flesh underlined by the earthiness of turned soil overwhelmed her. She was trapped and left to starve. Amora had outlived her purpose and killed the last enemy they had left. She hissed and threw her body against one wall then the other.

Wood cracked, but there was no give or sign of escape. They'd left her imprisoned to plummet deeper into insanity. Amora slid down the rough wall and splinters pierced the skin of her back. She curled into herself while wrapping her arms around her scraped bare legs. Her whimpers sounded pitiful and weak to her ears. Amora squeezed her eyes shut.

Was this a dream where she thrashed in her bed, bound in tangled sheets?

Part of her hoped she would awaken, the lingered fear and loss of control slow to fade. Although, the other half screamed this was the way it should end. Would it be a fitting punishment for all the crimes she'd committed?

Amora shivered, her whimpers built louder. They were sounds of a wounded animal and maybe that was what she was in the end—a helplessly trapped animal. She lashed out. Her fists repeatedly connected with the walls of her makeshift tomb. It's merely a dream—a nightmare—she will awaken in her motel room bed. She repeated a mantra of two simple words. Wake up, wake up, wake up, WAKE UP! With each utterance the back of her head painlessly connected with splintered slats. It was a dream, she needed to open her eyes and wake up.

* * *

AMORA'S WOUNDS SLOWLY HEALED, she'd fallen asleep the moment she'd landed face first in bed. As always, the nightmare that awakened her a mere hour before remained in her conscious brain. Thick, dark canvas and duct tape covered the few windows. As she'd slept, blood had dried and cracked on her skin. She had quickly removed the stiff fabric of her clothes and disposed of them and her boots in a black trash bag. Hot water ran in brownish-red rivulets down her body disappearing through the rusted ring of the drain.

Only an hour remained of sunlight, and then she would make the trip back to camp. Impatience made her irritable, and she longed for her club. An odd awareness of wrongness remained as if she'd lost a part of her. Her fists spasmodically clenched on the grimy tile and her nails dug deep into the cool stained surface. She tried to remember something or anything to explain the feeling. Amora lost much over the centuries, her family, mind, and freedom. Amora's instinct—a gut-deep reflex—was born and bred over brutal centuries, Amora learned not to ignore it.

Hot water prickled on the cusp of pain as it cascaded down her body. Each mark she bore was a remembrance, a story told in a visceral forget-me-not journey of ugly scar tissue. Just as she couldn't scrub away the marks, Amora couldn't escape the darkness of her thoughts. A mind continuously tormented by specters.

Each ghost more brutal than the one before and it pushed Amora closer to the precipice. She'd heard the supposed wise men say it was courageous to step back from the ledge. To have the courage to awaken another day to discover beauty within the shit-stained world. Amora knew there wasn't anything positive. She lived with a blinking neon target on her back and an almost obsessive desire to kill.

With a violent twist, she turned off the water and stepped from the shower then roughly dried off. The pads of her fingers brushed raised tissue here and there. Her head jerked toward the open bathroom door, she caught a familiar and torturous scent and heard the rattle of the doorknob. Subtle, her possible attacker wasn't. Amora dropped the towel as she silently made it to the door and she threw it open. A hiss of pain and rage exploded from her as sun caressed her forearm. The stench of burned flesh once again forced her back. Her fingers wrapped around the elegant column of a feminine throat.

A frightened squeak and violent pants passed Lark's pouted lips. She slammed Lark's back to the wall beside the door. A foreign instinct to protect—to cherish—warred with her need for survival. This was…she refused to let the thoughts form and then she had her distraction. A flash of black ink showed above the collar of Lark's shirt. Every piece of Amora froze as she ripped the fabric from the lightly tanned skin. Amora's knees nearly gave under her, and again she existed in Hell.

Lark gagged and gurgled, clawed at Amora's arm, and she only increased the pressure. Her other hand covered the black roses tattoo to discover the frantic rhythm. She had killed them all. No one should've survived to produce another generation.

A casual flick of her wrist and Lark sailed across the room where she landed beside the bed. Lark choked and gasped while she tried to breathe. She approached Lark calmly, an emotion she didn't feel and crouched down. Amora looked down at the mottled red face, the red-streaked white of her eyes. She slowly brought them face to face.

Lark's breathless pants were warm against her mouth. "I would begin explaining because very shortly, I will carve this—" She deliberately stroked the tattoo. "From your chest as a souvenir. While I am doing that, I will decide if your death will be quick or extremely slow."

"Please, just—" Lark cleared her throat as her voice broke. "I'm—" Amora cut her short with a menacing rumble.

"I know who the fuck you are."

"I found sanctuary with Seamus' pack. I and the others thought you were a rumor the Elders spun stories of. When—"

"I left that old basilica in ruin, no one survived," Amora spat out the accusation. She had destroyed it soul by soul, stone by stone and set the remains ablaze simply to watch it all burn.

"But the children were hidden away and protected by the Elders. The Order's numbers have grown, and the hunters are everywhere. I escaped, you have to believe that."

"I don't have to believe shit. What the fuck are you doing here? If it's not to attempt to do away with me as all your kind has done before, what's your angle, girl?" Amora demanded.

Lark appeared soft and too young to possess a killer instinct. Amora surged to her feet. She walked to her bag and pulled out clothes. She fingered the burn on her forearm before dressing with sharp movements. "Well, daylight is waning, and I need to get on the road. Besides, I still haven't decided if I'm going to kill you. This little tale of yours better be a good one."

"I worked in the archives at the monastery, and I came across... wait!" Amora darted a look over her shoulder as Lark crawled to retrieve the bag she hadn't noticed and dug through the contents. A book wrapped in a plastic bag appeared, Lark tried to hand it to her, but she refused to take it. The stranger angrily shoved the book back into the bag.

Amora was curious, yet Angelus Kali was a name she hadn't heard in a while. A Soul Collector clothed in the guise of an angel when he was anything but. The black roses that marked the cultists' flesh were the same that graced Kali's crest.

"He's a demon, not an angel as we were led to believe. We killed in his name, in the name of God, doing what we thought was good."

"Wake up call, huh?" The night she'd destroyed his house of syco-phants had started a bigger war. A series of bloody strikes over the centuries, she terminated his followers one bounty at a time. Turn-about being fair play, he hit at her in any way possible. Mostly through her son, Ripper, the young demon/vampire hybrid's presence was a smack in the old demon's face.

Kali's attempts to lure Ripper away from Amora always ended in failure. Amora couldn't help the amusement that came when she remembered the demon discovered her seduction of his son Demonus. As the last of her line, it was her duty to carry on, but in doing so, she'd also given birth to the next in Kali's line. She and Demonus had developed an odd kinship. He hated his father as much as Amora did.

"The hunters are striking, body counts are adding up and no matter the monster, innocents are dying."

"Monsters are not innocent. We won't openly live as one with the humans no matter the stupidity of the younger generations." Preter-natural creatures existed within the safety of secrecy, and human allies were few. In the last century, the optimistic idiotically spoke of treaties. "If you think it could happen, then you're deluded and child-ish. Hunters will exist long after The Order collapses and Kali fades back into the primordial ooze he belly-crawled from. Go home."

"Amora, you have…" Lark's warm, soft hands wrapped around her arm and she narrowed her eyes as she turned to the woman.

The shock of the tattoo was easing, and she could once more smell the irresistible scent of her skin. Feeling the monster ready to feed, to claim, she pulled away from Lark.

"I don't have to do a fucking thing. You want to go on some do-gooder campaign for the monsters of the world, fine. Although I can tell you right now, you won't get any help from me."

"But, Amora, please, there's no one—" Whatever Lark had been about to say ended abruptly and her chin met chest as silky dark hair concealed her face.

"You're right, no one 's going to join your crusade, especially me. We exist in the shadows for a reason. Now, go back to camp, Seamus doesn't like when his pack members stray and I'm sure he didn't allow you to see me alone."

"I'm not giving up, Amora, we're not done."

Amora chuckled at the stubborn determination that mixed with a good old-fashioned pout. The woman was cute if a little optimistic. Lark jerked the bag from the floor. There was one more glance at as the short, curvy Lark—her mate—disappeared out into the dying light of day. It wasn't true, it was another one of Kali's tricks, and she wouldn't succumb to his cruel games. Lark was a pawn like all the others, a promise of sweetness she'd stopped believing in during the days of her torture and enslavement.

CHAPTER 9

$\mathcal{L}$ark attempted to rub the chill from her arms. She hid in the shadows of Club Revenge. Amora had paid one more visit to Seamus and met with him and Ada briefly. Lark followed Amora home. New Orleans was strange and alien land compared to before. The presence of beasts of every kind stayed hidden within the shadows. Awareness of them was like an icy breath across her nape.

The world she knew for the past twenty years of her life was far different from the cities she'd traveled through the last six months. The stench of rot and evil clung to everything and everyone. She had tracked rumors of Amora Medina-Jackyl where they were the loudest.

Men and women leered at Lark, their eyes filled with desire as she watched the vamp from a distance. She needed Amora's help, or she wouldn't survive on her own. Vast amounts of knowledge collected within the walls of The Order of Angelus' archive, she'd studied everything she needed to know about the beasts she would encounter. Although, the Forbidden Tomes she'd stumbled across showed her the creatures they fought were far less dangerous than the human animals she'd known.

Amora's tall, slender body moved with innate grace. The beauty of Amora defied the bloody tales spun in hushed tones. Amora hid her

amber curls that reached her shoulders beneath her cap. The black of
Amora's t-shirt stood out starkly against her porcelain skin. Lark's
face flushed at the thought and brought her mind back to safer
subjects.

She needed the vampire's help, she didn't possess the strength or
experience to free her baby sister. Meadow recently celebrated her
fourth birthday, and it was a significant milestone within the doctrine
of The Order.

Harold and Sarah, her parents, were optimistic their youngest
would join the ranks of the Hunters. Lark's weakness of body, her
submissive and pacifist nature turned into a great disappointment for
her Hunter parents.

In the week she'd observed Amora, she'd discovered a surprising
development. The monster was capable of tenderness. Ada told
stories of the vamp washing her hair and being soothed with a
gentle embrace. That night, the interactions she'd witnessed
between boss and employees intensified her hope Amora would
agree to help.

She stroked her fingertips over the cracked glossy surface of a
photo in her pocket. She gathered all her courage to carry out the next
phase of her plan. With a single calming breath, she stroked her damp
palms down the sides of her skirt, and she took the first step with
determination. The crush of bodies parted, but she lost sight of
Amora for a moment until she broke through the crowd.

Amora instantly lifted her gaze from the drink she mixed, and a
knowing smirk pulled at one corner of her mouth. The tall woman
slid the beverage to the waiting customer then straightened and
crossed her arms under her small breasts. Black eyes tracked Lark's
every movement as she neared, her eyes fell to Amora's mouth, and
she shivered as she watched the tip of Amora's tongue swirl around a
deadly sharp fang. A memory came unbidden of what those sharp
incisors felt like on her skin, the needle prick sting and her thighs
trembled. Amora's sexy grin pulled wider, and her nostrils flared,
shame infused Lark's body as she realized Amora knew.

Lark eased onto a stool directly in front of Amora. Weak, unable to resist her unnatural desires for women and it was punctuated with blaring clarity by a sudden yearning for the creature before her.

"Hello, Amora." Her voice cracked as she wrung her fingers on her lap.

"Wondered when you'd stop stalking me. Hunter material you ain't."

Of that, she was well aware. She'd heard it enough over the years. Her weakness obvious, a natural reaction to flinch. She'd spent her entire life as a disappointment.

She knelt at altars of what she now knew were false idols to be blessed with the strength to fight. It never happened. They'd relegated her to a mere vessel for future generations.

"No, I was not afforded that honor."

"Good thing, I'd have killed you already." Lark flinched at the brutal honesty. "What do you want from me, Lark? I made myself quite clear at the motel."

"Same as I needed then, your assistance." Lark pulled the picture from her pocket and with trembling fingers slid it toward Amora. A light brow arched and a towel snapped from over Amora's shoulder as she wiped her hands before picking up the photo.

"Yours?" The voice was flat and dark eyes shuttered. Amora's knowing gaze searched for signs of fallacy.

"No, my sister, she's four, and her name is Meadow."

"And what does she have to do with any of this?"

"In a few years' time, she'll begin her training as a Hunter. I want you to get her for me."

"So, let me see if I got this right…"

Lark tried to hold her ground, but her natural reaction to retreat took over as Amora leaned onto the bar. The vamp's presence a tangible force in her space.

"You want the monster, me, to kidnap your sister and in turn, you throw me to the Hunters."

"No! Please!" Her voice trembled. "She's just a baby. I could give her a normal life. She's young enough to forget."

"And I'm the only one who can give you what you need?" There was more to the question than what was on the surface, but she couldn't read the emotions that played through Amora's gaze.

"You've defeated The Order before. I read the accounts of an Elder who briefly survived. You're a warrior, in the Forbidden records they say you are fierce, ruthless, and have destroyed many evil creatures. The Founders of our Order trained you, and you can't be defeated."

"Anyone can be beaten, Lark, it just depends on how badly you want to survive." Amora's cool fingertips danced along the back of her hand, and she gasped. "Did these books of yours detail exactly how your Elders trained me?"

Nausea rolled in her stomach, she remembered every word written and as much as she wanted to forget, her brain refused to release any information she'd read. "Yes."

"I was an attack dog, mindless with starvation and torture. What's in it for me to risk that again?" Amora waved her hand and looked around before looking back at her. "To put all this on the line for a girl destined to be a Hunter. Why shouldn't I just think this fucked-up plan of yours is nothing more than a trap? My proclivities for deli-cious..." Lark stopped breathing as Amora's gaze turned intense. "... feminine flesh is well-known, and you do fit the bill, darlin'." A thick Southern drawl took over Amora's voice. Lark noticed dependent on whom Amora spoke with, her dialect and inflection changed.

"I'll do or give anything to have Meadow." Her face flamed at what she realized she promised.

"Anything, even lay on the altar as a sacrifice to the monster your people created? You've probably never even lifted that skirt to show your beautiful pussy to anyone, and I'm not one for an amateur hour." What should have been relief at her words was instead a slap, and she dropped her eyes to her fingers laced in her lap. "Babe, cover me, I'm done for the night, I don't want to be disturbed."

"Sure thing, Boss, as soon as Tasha's off stage, I'll let her know she's closing. Have fun." The amusement in the other woman's voice made her head pop up to find Amora watched her.

"Let's go."

"Wh-where?"

"Upstairs to my place, we can talk a bit more..." Her eyes widened as Amora smirked and swirled her tongue around her fangs again. "...Privately." She wondered if that would be an appropriate time to run screaming and forget her foolhardy plan. "Let's go, Lark, I hate to repeat myself."

She swallowed hard, lowered her head as she hopped off the stool and walked to the end of the bar. Amora slipped from behind it, and her slender hand rested at the small of Lark's back. Was she supposed to feel like a lamb led to slaughter? Although, a thrill traveled her skin at the stroke of slender fingers along her spine. Amora's body crowded against hers. She was shaking by the time they entered Amora's place. The open loft apartment was huge, there were no walls and screens separated bedrooms from common areas, except the bathroom.

Lark froze inside the door at a line of painted portraits. They appeared to be Amora through the ages. She moved toward them and studied each one, most were of Amora scantily dressed as the women downstairs in what could be no more than undergarments.

"I was a Burlesque performer for a short time after my escape, sideshows and such. It's a profession where you're never in one place long. It can be profitable in its way."

"Do you still perform like the women downstairs?"

"No, I haven't been on stage for a very long time." Amora's tone was wistful. "I miss it, it's an art form. There's beauty in the tease. The mere glimpses of flesh, a curve of a breast." Lark spun as fingers stroked over the side of her breast. "The elegant curve of a throat." She shivered as tepid lips brushed her throat. "A peek at the curve of womanly hips." Amora's hands cupped the rounded curves of her hips as Amora's taller frame came flush against her back. "Before the reveal."

"I thought you weren't into amateur hour." Her lashes fluttered against her cheekbones. Lark attempted to hide her expressive eyes that always betrayed her thoughts and emotions.

"One body is good as another, baby, and you have to learn sometime." The hem of her skirt eased upward with a whisper of sensation on her skin as Amora fisted the sides.

"Is that all I would be, a body? I had thought—" Words ceased as Amora's fangs pricked her skin.

"I know what you thought, some romantic notion of first times and whispered words of love, but unlike a man, I won't lie. I won't make promises."

Her thighs quivered and tightened as a hand pushed roughly between her legs. Lark jerked away, fell back against the wall hard enough to shift one of the pictures and looked up at Amora.

"You, you can't treat—"

A cold laugh filled the room, and she went silent at the sound.

"Then don't offer yourself up like some sacrificial virgin, some of us don't live on high moral mountains. Some of us will merely take what's offered, and baby, it was offered." Amora spun away, and Lark tried to get her body under control. "Your scent is strong, you wanted it and don't deny you did."

The truth of that statement shook Lark to her bones. It wasn't just want, it was like a fire under her skin. All the fantasies she'd had in her lonesome bed crashed into her and threatened to push the oxygen from her lungs.

"I was told it was wrong and just another weakness. Being a great disappointment to my parents and The Order is not something I'm newly familiar with, and they planned to offer me as a womb. It's the reason I escaped." She shuddered in revulsion at the thought of Reginald and his touch, and the way his body trapped her between him and the library shelves. The things he'd whispered to her he would do to her made her sick.

"Who was he?"

Lark snapped her chin up at the demand, the cold, deadly look in Amora's eyes made her shiver. The emotion shaded in something else a reaction she couldn't understand.

"No one, just one of the Hunters, he had the most kills and was the highest ranking. He used to trap me and tell me things."

"Come away from the wall, Lark, I think you've learned your

lesson on consequences. Have you eaten?" Tenderness softened Amora's tone, the woman was a contradiction and Lark was fascinated by it. Lark straightened her skirt, approached Amora and her nose scrunched at the odor of blood.

"Unless you want to be my dinner, I suggest you get used to the smell." Humor laced the words, and she relaxed slightly. "Dinner?"

"What do you have?"

"I have takeout menus, vampires don't need to consume food, occasionally I like it though sickness be damned. I do drink a lot of blood and alcohol, neither of which will work as adequate sustenance for humans. Pick." A drawer opened, and a thick stack of papers appeared in front of her.

"I don't have a lot of money, this will—"

"I asked if you were hungry, not if you could afford it, pick, it's on me. We still have a conversation to have, and like I said downstairs, this needs to be private. What I do when I'm not here isn't for my employees to know."

She remained silent as she flipped through the menus and tried to figure out what most of them were. They had basic meals at the monastery and nothing fancy at the camp. She picked something unclear of what she'd ordered, but Amora made the call. Amora leaned back on the counter across the room and watched her. That cold stare seemed to see more than she wanted them too. It was disconcerting.

Knowing Amora through books, stories and rumors didn't compare to the reality of the vampire's presence. The briefest glance shifted from clearest blue to the darkest onyx stole her breath and made her traitorous body respond.

"You're wet."

The knowledge she couldn't hide her body's natural reaction embarrassed her, and she wanted to disappear.

"Is it the fact that I'm a woman or that I'm a taboo fuck?"

"You're a gorgeous woman. I have never been able to control what I..." She paused searching for the right word. "Like."

"I'm not beautiful, I'm scarred inside and out, I've more blood on my hands than all your Hunters combined. The killing doesn't bother me, I crave the taste of the fear I get when I feed. But do you know what I find even sweeter than the fear, Lark?" Oh, Amora's tone went all low and husky, that voice was a caress to her senses, and her body continued to weep. The space between her thighs warmed and tingled, and Amora's eyes closed and bared her fangs.

"What's sweeter?"

"You're still playing with fire. Lust, a need so strong it infuses the very essence flowing through your veins. You'll do well to control it, Lark. I may be able to resist that slight fear making your heart flutter wildly, but I won't guarantee the same of the allure of that cream gathering hotly between those rounded thighs."

She jumped as Amora pushed quickly from the counter and moved across the room. "Give this to the delivery person when they arrive, tell them to keep it." Money landed on the counter, she stiffened as Amora leaned down and her soft lips almost pressed to hers. "You're more tempting than any meal I have ever met." Lark ceased breathing, and her eyes went wide as Amora's tongue flicked over her mouth. Amora's strong fingers twisted roughly in her hair and jerked her head back. "Next time you offer, I won't show you any mercy. You'll be fucked and fed upon. You'll scream my name the whole time. I'll own you in every way possible."

The brush of cool lips was almost indiscernible before Amora was gone, she disappeared as if she had never stood beside Lark. Lark raised her hand to her mouth, traced the curves and sat there feeling lost. Fucked and fed upon, Amora would own her. What had she done? Would her heart and soul survive? Would her naivety remain intact or would she lose everything she had fled The Order to protect?

CHAPTER 10

Smoking flesh turned to ash and laughter met her screams. Her body bowed upward as she fought against the heaviness of the chains that secured her to the wall. Amora's screams and hisses turned to utterances of nonsense as she savored a moment's reprieve as a broad body blocked the single, narrow window. Paper-thin flesh cracked and blistered.

"Amora!" Her head thrashed with confusion, they never said her name with concern. Hell, they'd never called her by her name at all. Amora had barely remembered it or the before by the end. "Amora, please!" Terror, someone afraid for her, the sound was beautiful in the torturous day. A scream pierced the cell as fire licked at her body as her fingers and toes dug into soft, damp soil.

"You won't break me! I'll die first." She hissed with her last stores of rage. Agony stole a bit more of her mind. Soft hands stroked her face in a comforting touch.

"Amora, come back to me, please." The plea was soft as tender lips touched hers.

Dream and reality battled for supremacy, yet gentleness led her back from the precipice of darkness. Her crazed mind desperately tried to move closer to that voice that called to her and whispered to her of loving things. Strange hands seized her arms, and the chains broke as she circled a slender throat and squeezed. The slight pain of nail pricks caused her lids to slam open. Frightened wide eyes overwhelmed an ashen face stared at her and hands gripped her wrists.

"Lark!" She released the woman's throat and searched for damage, her fevered mind still lost partly in the past. "Are you insane? Never do that again." The monster and female warred inside her, one wanted to deny—to feed—and the other screamed to claim Lark as hers. She couldn't allow it. Too much remained at stake, Lark would always be in danger and was too young to find herself dragged into Amora's fucked-up life. She couldn't deny herself one taste —one night.

Her hands and fingertips caressed over Lark as the woman lay gasping on her bed. "Can you swallow?"

Her only answer was a jerky nod until Lark spoke in a rough and cracked whisper. "I heard you scream." Reality came back in a rush as she noticed her position. She lay between lush thighs. The t-shirt she'd let Lark borrow rested high on the sweet curve of her belly.

Lust gut-punched her, and she rested her weight on one arm as she pushed the hem higher. Lark's small breasts were bared in the dim shuttered room. Lark's tightly furled nipples were pale pink areolas that darkened to deep coral at the pointed peaks. She couldn't help but lick her lips as she lowered her head, flicked the hard tip of her tongue over one. The texture caused her to moan as Lark shivered and arched. "Pretty."

She lowered her head, wrapped her lips around the hard bud and rolled her tongue over it. Amora sank her fangs into Lark's tender flesh and tasted the perfect flavor of a few drops of blood. It was the heady flavor of lust perfectly infused with fear, and she increased the pressure for another taste. It was sweeter than the first.

Lark's thighs trembled and gripped Amora's hips. She angled her hips down and pushed her stomach to wet cotton that was warm where it met her cool skin. The strong scent of Lark's arousal made all others before pale in comparison. She sat up and rested back on her heels, Lark's thigh draped over hers, and she scored the satiny skin with elongated nails until she met the creases where thighs met panties.

"Is there nothing you're going to say? Perhaps tell me no?"

Lark's plump lips parted, but whatever she was going to say ended as Amora stroked her thumb across the crotch of the plain white panties. She lifted her thumb to dart her tongue out to sample Lark's unique flavor.

"Amora." A plea for her to stop or continue she didn't know. Lark's breathing was labored, her heartbeat thumped rapidly, and her hips moved restlessly.

"If you want it, you have to ask for it. I have fed from the unwilling, but in this…" Amora hooked her fingers in the fabric that hid the pussy she was helpless to resist, and she flexed her fingers until she heard the satisfying rip of fabric. "Oh, baby, has anyone ever tasted you?" Swollen lips parted to expose the tiny bud of Lark's clit, and the delicate inner lips and Amora lowered her gaze to find the glistening entrance. Her thumb circled it and pushed slightly into the tight heat.

"No, Amora, that feels…" Amora watched perfect white teeth sink into a pouty lower lip as Lark's hips canted to take more of her thumb. The muscles fluttered around the tip and Amora's lips pulled into a smirk. She pushed deeper and stroked the wet velvet of Lark's channel, and a small gasped whimper was music to Amora's ears.

Her need grew to ravenous levels as she grabbed Lark's wrist. Amora positioned her lover's hand between her thighs and Amora groaned at the picture before her. "Touch yourself, don't be shy, show me how you like that little bud of yours stroked." Honey-hued skin flushed pink with embarrassment before Lark began to move her fingertips in easy circles. "Such a good girl, don't stop."

She slid backward and laid on her stomach between Lark's thighs, and placed her palms under Lark's knees to push them toward Lark's chest. Her tongue slipped past her lips and slipped between Lark's fingers and doubled the pressure on her small clit. Lark jerked and then stopped. "I don't believe I told you to stop."

She licked Lark's flavor from her lover's fingers. "Keep going, and when you're about ready to come, I'll slide my tongue inside just to feel the way your pussy feels all tight around it." Index and middle digits held the flushed folds apart and danced teasingly along the sides of Lark's clit. Lark's curvy hips arched and rolled, the woman lost in her pleasure, yet she felt Lark held a part of herself back. She wanted all or nothing, she nipped at Lark's bud with the sharp edge of her teeth, and a keening cry split the air before being muffled.

Amora narrowed her eyes as Lark held her breath to suppress her sounds of pleasure. "I want them." Confused, hazy blue eyes met hers across the expanse of Lark's torso. "Moan, scream, beg, but don't hold back."

She wrapped her lips around the tender bundle of nerves, sucked gently and Lark's beautiful cry once again met her ears. Lark listened so well, eager to please and she had visions of discovering how much the young woman would give her. What limits she could push Lark passed and quickly tapped Lark with her tongue. Each lightning-fast movement caused Lark's body to arch and shake. Lark made sounds that bordered on the edge of panic. Amora refused to show mercy. She wanted the response, the rush of cream. But more than that, she wanted to feed on her as ecstasy coursed through Lark's veins.

Her fangs dropped farther as she sensed Lark's complete loss of control. She prepared to sink her fangs into the creamy skin of Lark's thigh. The soft skin had resisted for a mere moment before it gave beneath the sharp tips and a throat cleared destroying the spell.

"Am I interrupting?"

She cursed as Lark screamed and tumbled sideways off the bed.

"Boy, what the fuck are you doing here?" Ripper stood in the opening between the screens and smiled smugly at her. She stood and grabbed her jeans from the end of the bed, slipped them on, and then reached for her shirt. "Um, you can wait in the kitchen."

"Really, you never worried about me seeing dinner before."

"Get the fuck out." The tone of her voice broached no argument and Ripper chuckled as he turned.

"Who-who was that?"

"That, baby, is my kid." She slipped the shirt over her head and walked to the side of the bed where Lark peeked over the edge. Amora bent down and brushed a kiss to Lark's mouth. "Bathroom is through there. After I get rid of him, we will finish this." Lark merely nodded and warily watched the opening where Ripper disappeared.

Amora closed her eyes and counted to ten, and then she walked out of her bedroom. "Haven't we talked about this penchant of yours?"

He chuckled, and she curled her hands into fists. "Yeah, yeah, no unannounced visits. Ma, you didn't have to stop on my account, I could have waited, for a turn to feed." Ripper leaned his lean body against the wall outside the kitchen and watched her with dancing green eyes.

"Don't even think about it, one finger touches her, son or not, I will rip your arm off." The possessiveness shocked her, and her eyes narrowed before she hid the reaction. She never became attached, and Lark would turn out no different.

"So violent and possessive of the new toy."

She growled, and her son chuckled as he held his hands up backing away to turn into the kitchen.

"Play with your mate and leave Lark alone." She followed and watched him pour blood into the warmer.

"Mate, Ma, is there something you want to tell me?"

She laughed, it was a raw and foreign sound, as Ripper waggled his brows.

"Don't deflect."

"When you use all those fancy words, you're giving yourself away. Can't camouflage that proper upbringing when you let the Southern badass fade. *Y'all* and *goin' to*, even throw in an *I don't rightly know* or even an *I'ma fixin' to*."

"You're an ass, and I ask again as you ignored me earlier, what are you doing here?"

"Can't I visit my lovely mother just because I miss her?"

He was up to something, and that question just proved it. Amora narrowed her eyes as he looked passed her, his lips turned up into a charming, nearly innocent smile. Tentative fingertips touched her back, and Lark looked around her arm at Ripper.

"So, shy, almost virginal." She shot Ripper a glare and the boy had the nerve to feign a fainting spell. "Mother, you have found the great Societal Unicorn, a virgin, I'm nearly jealous, they're nearly extinct or jailbait. She is legal, right?"

"Fuck you, she's twenty."

Ripper's brow rose skeptically. "Are you sure? Did you check I.D.? Besides, Ma, big difference between four-hundred-and-two years and a mere twenty. Have you done the deed?" Amora glared at her son hoping he'd drop the unwanted line of questioning. "Wow, can I play with her? You're not exactly equipped to bust that cherry."

"I'm more than equipped, have you seen Tasha yet?" Anger flashed through Ripper's gaze before he concealed it and turned back to his lunch prep.

"Low, Mother, very low. Actually, I need to talk to you in private, if you could put your toy away, we can talk."

She turned to find Lark nervously chewing her bottom lip. "Why don't you take a shower, get dressed." Lark left after giving her a nod. "This better be good, Ripper, I've had a shit week."

"Oh, Ma, it's about to get worse."

CHAPTER 11

$\mathcal{T}$he curses and raised voices from the kitchen made her flinch. Lark sat on the edge of the bed, tried to block out the rage and let her mind return to what almost happened. Fire licked at the apex of her thighs at the sensory memories of Amora's tongue flicking over her. The words Amora had spoken replayed inside her head and fueled fantasies, and transformed the vague fantasies she'd used in the past into vivid mental picture shows.

She hadn't completely understood the reality of what being with a woman entailed until she'd discovered the talented ministrations of Amora's tongue. Her nipples tightened into aching points as she remembered Amora's fangs barely piercing the flesh of her breast, yet she wanted more. What would it be like to feed the beautiful Amora? Lark's thighs trembled, and she squeezed them together, she was so close to falling, and Amora had scarcely touched her.

A door slamming brought her back from her thoughts and Ripper, Amora's son, appeared in the opening between screens. Fear infused her veins, and she dropped her chin to her chest.

"Nothing to be frightened of, Lark, no wonder my mother is possessive, I'm almost jealous of her claim."

"She hasn't made—"

"Yes, little one, she has, she may not have bitten you, but her scent is all over you. She'd kill anyone that laid a fingertip on you, and that includes me. Well, she would merely cause me a bit of damage. I am her son after all. Are you hungry?"

"Not really."

"Let's go out, take a walk in the sun. Let you enjoy it while you can." She didn't understand what he meant by that, but she stood, and she walked a wide berth around him as she headed for the door. "Let's go out back, Ma's downstairs and she needs some time to cool off."

"What happened?"

Ripper didn't answer her question merely opened a door and motioned her out into the late afternoon sun. Once they reached the bottom of the metal steps and started walking out of the alley, he broke the silence.

"Do you know who my grandfather is?"

She shook her head as she darted a glance at him.

"Angelus Kali. My mother in her great and twisted wisdom, seduced Kali's son, I don't think that was in the books you read. Yes, Ma filled me in a bit."

"You're? But you're, how?" She realized they were walking in the sun and hadn't even thought of the consequences. There was a lot she didn't know, as always, her brain began to pick apart information she'd absorbed and attempted to decipher the problem.

"Demon and vampire combined, but the demon side is a bit stronger. I'm a rather dirty little secret for the great Kali."

"Doesn't he claim you as family?"

"Oh no, little one, my existence is a slap in the face. My parents shared a mutual hatred for Kali and from loathing, they created me. A perpetual dig, Amora and Demonus, well, they didn't think of the result only of what insult my birth would bring."

"End result?"

"I'm next in line for Kali's so-called throne, I won't have a choice, with Kali's expiration, I will ascend. It's the only reason he retired back to the murky depths he appeared from, Amora is giving me a little more time of freedom from becoming a parasite."

"Parasite?"

"Yes, Kali exists on the souls he collects and controls. They feed him, are essential for his existence, and once I take over, it'll be my only means of survival. I'll inherit the souls he owns, but will also have to collect my own. It's a nasty business really, and I'm not ready."

"What happened?"

"My grandfather has decided to come out of hiding, it's been awhile since Amora and Kali have traded jabs, seems Gramps has decided it's time."

"But-I-I asked Amora."

"I know what you asked, and she informed me she's going to do it. The mission is a dumbass move, she's going to get herself captured or killed, I'm hoping for killed. She barely survived the last capture mentally intact, I fear this time she's fucked."

"She didn't tell me she was doing it. I don't want..." Lark rubbed her arms and took a deep breath. "I read about what they did, but today she had a nightmare, and it was—"

"I grew up hearing them, she'd never spoken of them, and she doesn't have to. Her scars tell the story of her hell well enough. So, your sister grows to be a Hunter, kills a few dozen, maybe she doesn't ascend to the esteem ranks of a sanctioned murderer, either way, is my mother's soul worth her rescue?"

Lark hadn't thought of what it would cost Amora to carry out the mission. "I can tell her that I don't want her to do it, I'll figure out another way. Maybe I could just go back, at least I can be near Meadow then."

"Too late, Lark, it's already been decided. Amora will get Meadow for you, no matter the danger. I just hope you can live with the consequences if this little venture blows the fuck up."

They ate and kept to safer topics, but her mind never stopped spinning with all the what-ifs that could likely play out. Ripper treated her as an old friend. However, it didn't change the troubled nature of her thoughts.

A shift in subjects changed the direction of the conversation. All the questions she wanted to ask flitted through her mind. The worst-case scenarios of Amora reliving the stories she'd read. Could she allow Amora to take that risk?

The sun was beginning to set as they walked back into Amora's home. Her brows furrowed finding another woman in Amora's arms, a stranger barely dressed and tucked in the space created by the vamp's thighs as she sat on the back of the couch.

"Dial down the jealousy." She scowled at Ripper's amusement.

"Tasha!" The man moved with blurring speed and swung the stranger into his arms.

"Baby boss, Amora told me you were here." She smiled as the woman named Tasha cuffed Ripper on the back of his head. "Put me down, you know I hate being manhandled."

"Why? You know you can't resist me, Tasha, let's get me drunk so I can inappropriately try to seduce you."

Tasha giggled as Ripper threw her over his shoulder and the two disappeared through the door leading downstairs.

"Enjoy your time out in the sun?" The question was sharp-edged, and the look in Amora's eyes sent a chill through her.

She cleared her throat. "Your son was surprisingly nice and gentlemanly."

"He has his moments. Did he touch you?" The coldness chilled her further, and apprehension danced down her spine. Amora's eyes turned black and unreadable.

"No, we simply went for a walk, and he bought me a meal." She remembered the night she'd met Amora, the feeling of being the prey of a hunt, but the terror she'd felt that night paled in comparison to the way Amora's darkened stare made her feel right then.

"Lark, come here."

The command forced her feet to move. She stopped a short distance from Amora, the vamp's hands gripped her hips and jerked her forward. A high-pitched squeak pierced the tense cloud that made the air in the room suffocating. Her hands came to rest high on Amora's chest, and she kept her eyes averted.

"Ripper will watch over you in my absence."

"I don't want you to go. I'll return home and accept my fate."

A growl jerked her eyes upward. "This isn't up for discussion; you'll do as I say. You started this, and it'll be finished. My son will protect you while I'm gone. I'll return with your sister, if I don't come back, Ripper will help you start a new life."

"Amora, it's too great a risk, he and I talked about it. I was selfish too—" Amora's mouth equal parts hard and soft slammed onto hers, and any argument she was about to make was forgotten as desire zinged along her nerves. Amora's tongue pushed inside and slid along hers. She moaned as slender fingers slipped under the waistband of her skirt and pushed it over her hips. It fell to pool around her feet. "Someone—" Amora's fangs nipped her bottom lip, and a fire ignited low in her belly.

"He's distracted by the mate he refuses to claim." Her t-shirt and bra quickly joined her skirt, and she stood between Amora's thighs in just panties. The sharp edges of Amora's nails scored her exposed flesh. She trembled and gasped as she watched the progression of Amora's nails. The red scratches burned slightly, her back arched as Amora's nails dragged over her nipples and her knees nearly buckled. "I did say that we would finish what we started earlier, didn't I?"

Lark nodded, completely lost within the unfamiliar and frightening sensations. Men had touched her before, nothing like this, but their touches never made her feel as if her skin was too tight.

"Frightened?" Amora pressed her nose to her throat and inhaled.

"Ner-nervous." The half-truth left an acidic taste on her tongue. Fear gripped her in a stranglehold and another stronger emotion —desire.

"Liar, so innocent." The huskiness of Amora's voice caressed her just as surely as the palms that moved over her bottom. Amora squeezed and tugged her closer.

Amora teasingly brushed kisses against her lips, jaw and throat, it increased the quivering of her body. She was naked while the woman remained fully clothed.

"Oh!" Amora opened over her left nipple and suckled, then pulled back to graze the hardened flesh with her teeth. Her hands went to Amora's shoulders, and her nails dug into her skin through the cotton of a t-shirt, a growl sounded and Amora bared her fangs. An emotion scary and improper made desire pull tight in the pit of her stomach.

"Shift, those rounded thighs to open, now." Without a shred of modesty, she shifted her feet, so different from earlier, Amora treated her as if she were delicate.

"I thought you'd be…" Her teeth sunk painfully into her lower lip as fingertips stroked the strip of cotton between her thighs. The caress barely there, but she felt it like lightning strikes to her senses.

"Not the first time, I won't promise to be gentle, but you'll come for me and only me. Listen well, decide now, because once I have you, no one else will. Mine in body and soul, to do with…" Her eyes slammed shut as fangs carefully nipped at the side of her neck. "As I see fit. I will own every moan, whimper and demand for release."

"I just thought I would be a body. You make it sound as if I will be your…" She ended the question. "You were lying to me and taunted me about my romantic notions." Amora chuckled, and the rough sound took her by surprise.

"I'm a bitch, Lark, often cruel and unapologetic, I love a soft, feminine form. Yours fits the bill quite nicely." She shivered again at the husky tone. "I still taste you, and I crave more, I'll have it until we grow tired of each other. If that be after a few hours or a few decades, you'll be mine until I say otherwise."

She whimpered as Amora's hand cupped her mound fully, fingers lying along her folds. Her touch was never that intense. Amora increased the pressure. Even with the fabric that separated and muted the sensation, her jaw went slack, and her eyes rolled.

All pleasure ceased as she felt cold steel against her hip and she opened her eyes as a lethal blade glinted in the dim light. It slipped under the side of her panties, and the fabric gave with a whisper of sound.

"Amora?"

"Easy, baby, the first rule you'll learn…no panties." She felt the rumble of the statement against her breast before Amora began to suckle with hard suction. Sharp painful pricks then the rumbling became louder. Cool air met Lark's overheated skin as the last of her cover disappeared, and Amora's fingers thrust fast and deep. Amora's palm stung her slit as it connected with her wet flesh. She cried out at the exquisite bliss of the slight pain.

The pain had never been part of her fantasies, but the piercing of fangs and the hard plunge of two fingers taking her untried body stole her breath and sanity. Her fingers carded through the silky strands of Amora's hair and the force of the bite increased. She shook, whimpered and begged incomprehensible utterances. Two digits became three, and the burn of unaccustomed stretch made her forget to breathe.

Amora pulled back, her tongue licking over Lark's skin where she knew the marks of fangs and teeth were. "Someone likes it rough. Do you like to be fucked? Answer me."

She arched her body fully into Amora's taller frame as fingers found a heart-stopping spot inside her. Tapping and rubbing, ruthlessly playing her with superior experience. Quick fumbles of her fingers never came close to that. Sweat misted her skin, her muscles rigid on the razor's edge of extreme euphoria. She let out a keening cry as a hand connected to her butt, and she locked her thighs around Amora's hand. Forcing her passion-heavy lids open to find Amora her with lips tinted crimson and eyes onyx with no hint of white. A dangerous smile pulled her lips tight, instead of trying to flee, she brought her lips to Amora's mouth.

The taste of her blood on Amora's tongue should have repulsed her not caused her to tighten around Amora's fingers. "I shouldn't— you—this isn't—" She spoke against those soft lips as she loathed to pull away. She clawed at the shirt that separated their skin, and her palms found the hard peaks of Amora's unrestrained breasts.

A great roar filled her ears seconds before Amora took her mouth, thrusted in time with the fingers that moved rough and deep. A slight twinge of pain forgotten and ignored. Strange whimpered moans muffled by Amora's mouth were pushed out with each pummel of fingers, the sharp snap of skin against her inflamed bud.

She arched abruptly into the thrusts as the kiss stole all rational thought and she clawed at the slender body pressed against her. The wet sounds of the fingers pushing roughly into her weeping body rang in her ears. The knot in her lower belly tightened, and heat flared beneath her skin. It was more than she could take, but she wanted more. She felt separate from herself, foreign, as if the person she was before Amora no longer existed. Amora's hand gripped her hair brutally and wrenched her head back, she tried to recapture Amora's lips, but the tug caused her scalp to burn.

"You're going to come for me." The voice that spoke wasn't the husky, smooth caress, but hard-edged with possessiveness. She didn't have a chance to speak before Amora's fangs sank deeply into the skin that surrounded her nipple. Pain morphed into a pleasure she'd never knew existed and slipped into a space of euphoria. Drugged and languid, and then the explosion happened. A great rush as her body clamped around Amora's fingers, a flood of hot wetness flowed heavily between her thighs. She held tight to Amora, frightened, light-headed, and she floated as her body relaxed. Her breathing labored as she shook, she listened to the moans and the animalistic sounds as Amora fed.

Owned, she felt as if she finally belonged, and pleasure faded as a sense of sadness and fear took over. What had she done?

CHAPTER 12

*R*ipper sat with his feet propped on her desk, and Amora was getting damn tired of him. "What the fuck is wrong with you? You've got ass readily available, and you're still fucking cranky." She glared at her son across the expanse of her desk as she reached out and pushed at his boots. The chair tipped backward, and she smiled coldly at the warning sound of a rattle.

Her son glared at her with his eyes peeking over the edge of her desk. She arched a challenging brow, and she dared the little shit to try something.

"If you had a will, I'd throw you into the sun."

"I've already promised everything to Tasha." Green eyes widened, and nictitating lenses blinked, nearly transparent secondary lens covered each eye. The whole serpent thing freaked her out, Demonus had mostly kept that form hidden. Ripper did it again. "Stop that!"

"Something wrong, Mommy Dearest?" She stretched out a rubber band, let it go and shot him the eye. "Dammit! What the fuck, Ma?" She chuckled as he grabbed his eye, glaring at her.

"Quit being a pussy, you ain't going to lose it. Do it again, and I'll take out the other one, this time I'll make sure you can't heal."

"I think you need to go fuck your mate and work off some of that frustration."

She growled at him, and he smirked at her realizing he'd hit a nerve. "Lark's not my mate." Denying it caused her molars to clench.

"Bullshit someone who you didn't raise to be exactly like you. You can deny it to everyone else, but not me and especially not yourself."

"She regrets giving in to the monster." Her pride stung admitting it. As she'd fed, Lark's lust turned to fear, and she had tasted the bitter regret. Lark couldn't hide emotions from her, she sensed it all in the rush of coppery sweetness over her taste buds. That strong sense of shame angered her, and she'd left Lark standing there. Rage burned through Amora's veins and squeezed her stomach in an unrelenting fist.

"Wow, that whole forbidden, creature of the night fuck thing always worked in your favor. The club opens in a few hours find another, you were never attached to a meal before." Ripper spoke as if it was easy. She'd always resisted the lure. No one had ever called to her before and made her thirst insatiable until she claimed her. She sneered as her son started laughing and it increased in volume until he was bent over with tears rolling down his face.

"I will kill you." That only made him laugh louder if that was possible.

"Ma, you did the whole Medina-Jackyl claim for life thing. Oh, this is going to be fun. Does she know?"

Of course she wasn't going to tell the innocent, mortal Lark about the family tradition. She still remembered the nights of learning the stories repeatedly to one day pass down. She'd avoided the whole mate thing as long as possible and only just realized where the compulsion came from the night she'd hunted Lark. She shook her head violently. Her son sobered at the look on her face, but it didn't last long. The gleam in his eyes she knew too well.

"You did hear that I will kill you." Ripper surged to his feet, and his hands shot out to grab her face, a broad, mischievous grin mocking her. He pinched her cheeks, and she sneered.

"Aw, it's finally happened, you're all grown up! When's the big date? Will I have brothers and sisters? Please, I've always wanted to be a big brother!"

She grabbed his wrists in a steely grip and pushed him, he flew backward to hit the door, rattling pictures on the walls beside it.

"We're going to play that one, huh? You've got your panties all in a bunch, well, bring it, Old Lady, I kicked your ass last time."

She snorted as she stood at a lazy pace and reached up to remove her hat tossing it on the edge of her desk. "You didn't kick a fucking thing, boy, still wet behind the ears and you hit like a fucking mortal."

He backed up toward the door, Ripper watched her with iridescent eyes as he moved never giving her his back.

The narrow hallway turned into the open space of the main room. She removed the dress shirt that covered the men's white tank, and they paced around each other. They each waited for the first strike to come from the other. A battle they both craved and couldn't resist. Like mother like son.

Ripper's feral grin matched hers, his skin rippled transitioning from tan to smooth onyx scales shimmering with hints of green. "I will show you *hits like a mortal.*" The battle began, well-matched, meeting blow for blow, kick for kick. The ripping of flesh as his claws hooked her side and she laughed as she spun bringing the back of her fist against the side of his face.

Momentarily stunned, he shook his head and surged forward. He kept his full demon in check, and she was well aware that if he didn't, she wouldn't stand a chance. Fangs stayed sheathed, acidic venom dripped on her forearm as she threw a quick succession of jabs. She growled at the pain as she lost a layer of skin, a rough laugh issued from Ripper's throat and he hissed. His arms shot out and grabbed hers, and she braced herself for the slam to a support pillar.

"Put her down right this minute!" In slow motion, Ripper and Amora turned their heads to find Lark standing on the sideline with her hands fisted on her hips.

"But—" Amora felt a sense of amusement as the little woman pointed a finger at her scaly ass son as if it were a normal occurrence. Her mate lifted a brow as she glared at Ripper.

"No buts, young man, put her down." The woman stomped her cute little foot, and Amora swallowed a snort.

"Ma, does she know I'm nearly two centuries older than her?"

"Son, I don't think she cares."

"God, you get a mate, and we can't have any more fun! Fuck, I don't want a stepmom, she's mean!" Ripper set her down, and she lifted her hand to rub the back of it across her split lip. Her son shifted from demon to angel in the span of a blink. To look at the angelic features, the masculine perfection so much like his father's, no one would ever guess the depraved reality beneath.

"Another woman who doesn't find you charming, it's why I lo— like Tasha and Lark so much. I knew there was a reason."

"Don't think I didn't catch that, watch those slips of the tongue, Ma, someone might think you have a heart." Her fist connected with his hard abs and he bent over as she slipped from her spot between him and the pillar.

"Look at you, can you do anything without fighting?" Her arm shot out to wrap around Lark's waist as she asked the question.

"You know I can, I'll even let you kiss 'em and make 'em better before I taste." She smirked at her mate's cheeks turning pink. Her hand slipped between Lark's thighs as she nipped at her mate's lips and a throat cleared. Darting a glare over her shoulder to find her son scrunching his nose at them and she nodded toward the door.

"Um, I would rather my parents not get freaky in front of me, you've scarred me enough. I'm going to my room!" Ripper stomped off, and she rolled her eyes at the smile he failed to hide before disappearing upstairs.

"We need to clean these up, Amora." Lark's fingertips traced the superficial bruises and cuts. The warm touches were caring and gentle. "If I asked you something would you be completely honest with me?"

"Depends on what you ask. Some topics aren't up for discussion." Lark nibbled nervously at her bottom lip, and she took over, sinking her teeth into the lush lower curve. A shuddered breath flowed shakily over her mouth, and she lifted Lark into her arms carrying her toward the bar. She placed her on the edge of it and looked slightly up as she pulled her lips away. "You had a question?" Amora smirked at the dazed look in her mate's eyes and loved the flush that tinted her skin. She lifted her hand to stroke her fingertips over the warmth of her pink cheeks.

"Why does Ripper call me your mate?" Shit, she would rather answer anything else, but Lark's insecure body language proved she needed an answer.

"He's a little shit that likes fucking with people."

"Oh," Lark uttered, she almost sounded disappointed. "What are mates?"

"Call it fate or biology, whatever. They reward the monsters for some reason. Some preternatural search their entire existences for that one. I never looked, because I figured Fate fucked me over per usual." She dragged her nose up the side of Lark's neck and drew in the perfume that was all Lark. A sense of peace settled heavily over her. She needed to change the subject, to deny the truth pushing to the surface. That was the one thing she could allow—pleasure and nothing more.

"You know the first time I caught your scent, the fear with the spice of arousal?" Her fingers circled Lark's ankles and stroked upward, teasing the hollows behind her knees and along her outer thighs. Fingertips met the edge of cotton. "Lark, what was the rule?"

"But...I...Amora, I couldn't just." Lark sighed and turned away. "I can't walk around without panties under my skirts."

"I'll keep cutting them off until you have none left."

"Amora, but—" Lark heavily sighed as Amora stopped the words by hooking her fingers in the side of the offending cloth and ripped them.

"Lark, I made myself clear. I think your offense warrants punishment." Lark's eyes went wide at her statement, and her mate shook her head.

"Pun-punishment? Amora, that's highly unnecessary and improper, I'm not a child." Amora ran her hands over Lark's womanly curves and groaned as she looked into Lark's eyes. She watched Lark's lids grow heavy. The scent of her woman's arousal thickened the air, and she jerked the fabric from Lark's body to drop it to the floor.

"No, baby, there is nothing child-like about you, but that doesn't excuse you disobeying. Now, you're going to hop off the bar and come with me." Her tone dared Lark to argue further.

She heard Lark's heart kicked into overdrive, need and a slight hint of fear filled Amora's nose. Her fangs dropped, and her nostrils flared as she helped her mate slip from the bar. Holding tight to Lark's trembling fingers, she released her to take a seat on a chair in front of the stage.

"Lift your skirt and lay across my lap."

"Amora!" She smiled as she inhaled the spice of Lark's excitement. "You can't mean to spank me."

"That's exactly what I mean to do. Do as you're told." Patience was a hard-earned skill, and she used it to await her mate's submission. Lark wouldn't tell her no, it was there in the increased heat of her mate's body and the dilation of pupils that drove out the pretty blue of Lark's eyes.

"This is most embarrassing."

"Quit protesting, I know your pussy is already wet for me." She lowered her voice. "Do I have to tell you again?" The petulant pout of Lark's sexy lips pulled Amora's nipples taut and the scent of her arousal mixed with that of her mate's scent.

She watched as Lark slowly shifted the pretty pale peach skirt with a predatory stare. It moved upward exposing smooth, lightly tanned calves, cute slightly dimpled knees and she bit her lips at the sight of round, soft thighs. She patted her lap as Lark breathed with quick puffs and the fabric finally bared the generous flare of hips.

"Beautiful." The gravelly tone was thick with desire as the soft curve of Lark's stomach came to rest on her lap. The underside of Lark's plump breasts nudged along her left thigh. "Such a good girl. You're perfect." Amora fully exposed the curves of Lark's ass as she pushed the fabric to her waist.

Her palm moved with tender caresses, smiling as Lark jumped when she neared the pretty, swollen lips of Lark's pussy. Lifting her hand, hesitating as her mate held her breath and then the palm of her hand connected. Lark squeaked, yet she only had eyes for the sexy bounce of ample curves, she repeated the smack to one cheek and then the other, repeatedly. Amora soothed the reddening, pale skin, as Lark's cries became moans. The strong scent of her mate's arousal was thick.

"Did we learn our lesson?" The question slipped from her lips at the same time she cupped Lark's soaked pussy. "Or do you need another?" She pushed her thumb into Lark's clenching heat. Fucking her in shallow thrusts as whimpers and hips arched showing her how much her mate wanted more.

A growl rumbled in her chest as nails pricked her thigh through the fabric of her jeans. She fisted dark silken waves and pulled until Lark knelt between her thighs. Slamming her mouth down onto Lark's bearing the faint imprint of teeth and blood burst upon her tongue as she stroked over her mate's lips. Amora's pushed inside, tongues tangled as the kiss turned frantic and rough. Shy fingers moved delicately over her skin, and she craved to strip Lark down, fuck and claim her fully this time. She tore her mouth from Lark's and scanned the flushed features, the sexy heavy-lidded stare. "Strip."

Lark seemed to want to argue but changed her mind as she straightened and stood in front of Amora. Clothes began to disappear exposing the beauty of lush curves and creamy skin. Amora reached over her head and grabbed the back of her shirt, jerking it over her head as she stood. Her fingers dropped to her belt. "Amora?"

"Only fair, baby." She kicked off her boots and stripped her jeans down her legs. Standing there every scar exposed in the stage spotlights. Her fingers clenched into fists as warm, satiny skin pressed to her cooler body and fingertips stroked over thick scar tissue.

"I remember every word." Words were breathy caresses across her chest, then nipples as Lark's lips blazed a trail of intense pleasure over her skin. Amora tensed as fingertips stroked lightly over the uneven patches where her skin never healed completely from the fiery rays of sunlight. "I-I used to dream of you, they told us stories of your hunger for women. Shame, always felt shame—" Lark words ceased as lips wrapped tight around her nipple and she sunk her fingers deep into her mate's hair. Amora was always the aggressor, rarely allowed anyone to touch her and the reality of letting someone else have reign over her was oddly wonderful. More frightening than a battle promising imminent death.

Delicate, the innocent woman treated the vicious creature as if she would break. Small hands settled on her hips in uncertainty. Lark's tongue flicked over her nipple then suckled gently. There was no heat, no uncontrollable lust brought on by the need to feed. This was something else, unfamiliar, and she needed to regain control.

Dropping one of her hands, she wrapped her fingers around Lark's wrist and moved it between her thighs. The first touch of her mate's fingers caused her to hiss and clench her jaw. It had been too long since she'd allowed anyone to touch. She normally found her release in the rush of copper over her tongue as she sated her hunger. It was an achingly light contact, a barely there push against her clit. Tightening her fingers in Lark's hair, she regretfully pulled her woman's mouth away from her nipple, but quickly lowered her head to nibble at the soft curves.

Desire built in great waves pushing at the edges of her control. She arched her hips, taking her mate's whimpers into her mouth as she pushed into the space created by Lark's parted thighs. A shudder worked through the woman in her arms, and she dipped her hand into the wet, heated slit to slide two fingers in deep. Lark arched pushing back. "So wet, I still remember how sweet you tasted." She groaned the words against Lark's mouth.

Lark touch faltered only for a moment before starting a slow circle on her clit. She thrust in and out, relished the ripple of Lark's silken sheath. Her gums stung as they receded, her fangs dropped as she quickly found the accelerated beat at the side of Lark's throat. The sharp points of her fangs pierced the skin with a slight resistance. Her cunt clenched tight as the first rush of lust-infused thickness over her tongue.

Muscles tensed as she wrapped her arm tight around Lark's waist and lifted her turning in a blur of motion. She laid Lark on the shiny black surface of the stage, rested heavy between her thighs as she forced her left hand between them. She plunged fingers fast and deep, her thumb began a punishing circle. Lark's nails dug into her back, searing as they broke through and she rode Lark's shaking form. Drinking deep as her mate writhed, whimpered and begged. The words came muffled as if from a distance as still she pushed, felt the cresting of the wave as she drove her mate higher.

Her name repeated in wild tones as Lark's heartbeat roared in her head. Wetness flowed heavy from Lark's pussy, sex-slicked sounds and still, she fed. Just as the pleasure reached its peak, Lark screamed, and her mate's orgasm became her own. She felt every ounce of desire and pleasure, her nipples ached, and her cunt clenched as Lark came with another rush of fluid around her fingers. Pulling out her fangs, she licked the crimson stain of blood from the lightly tanned skin as her mate held her tight, desperately trying to hold her, but she had no intention of moving away.

She kept her fingers inside Lark, savored the spasms around the digits as she rested her forehead between soft breasts. Amora lovingly brushed her lips over the inner curves. There was an odd tingling in her chest, an unfamiliar sensation, it felt like peace and contentment. With the feeling also came regret, she would leave Lark to give her mate what she wanted. If anything, she always went with her gut, and she had a feeling she wouldn't return.

CHAPTER 13

*S*ome scars were smooth fragile flesh beneath the pads of her fingers. Others thick and textured, yet the ones most damaging existed deeper than the cool pale skin nestled to hers. When the sun set Amora would leave, and as many times in the night as she'd asked Amora to stay, she was distracted by kisses and touches. The explanation on mates played through her head. Mate, the words thought in silence quickened her heart rate, what would it be like to have Amora as only hers. The monster they'd been taught to fear, Amora Jackyl, the boogeyman to The Order's children belonged to her.

For one day, Amora slept peacefully, no screams or cries for mercy intermingled with defiance broke the tranquility of the room.

"You care." Her head popped up and met green eyes that shined with an emotion akin to compassion. Whether that was for her or Amora, she didn't know.

"Yes, she's beautiful and possesses a tenderness she hates people to see." Lark kept her voice low despite knowing Amora wouldn't awaken until the sun began to fade behind the horizon.

"Don't believe in fairy tales, Lark. You're in bed and most likely in lust with a monster, a scourge to your precious Order." The silence stretched out for a few moments as Ripper stepped farther into the room and stopped beside the bed. "Do you truly know what they did to her?"

"I read." A menacing rumble of sound made her cringe.

"I don't give a fuck what you read, do you know? Have you ever known hunger, thirst, so great you'd sell your soul to slake it?" Her eyes burned as she shook her head, but he continued to speak. "The horror of watching your flesh turn to ash and fall to the bloody soil, can you even imagine what that does to you? What about seeing your parents murdered for an agenda of a vengeful demon or watching your home burn with your siblings inside?" Lark dropped her gaze to Amora's face and held her a little tighter as Ripper continued. "She relives that every fucking day, remembers the thirst and pain, existing alone in a mental hell she can never escape. I love my mother, we don't say it aloud often, but we say it in our way. She made me what I am through a fucked-up mistake of genetics and nurturing. Strong, so I'd never understand her loss."

"But you do understand."

"Yes, I do. But also, I understand if she carries out this plan of hers, to rescue a child important to her mate, she may not come back. I fear what they'll do to her this time will break the little sanity she has left. Can you live with knowing your request will do that to her?"

"I've tried to talk her out of it. I would go back home in a second to save her from that possibility, yet she refuses to allow me."

"Of course she does, everything in Amora is screaming for her to protect what is hers. She will lay her life on the line for you as quickly as she would me. We are all the family she has left. If she doesn't come back, it will be up to me to take care of you."

"Why would you do that? I'm nothing, just a foolish woman that asked her to risk her life."

"Because you are my mother's, and we take care of our own."

"Why are—what are—" She didn't know how to ask the question.

"One day, Kali will fall, it could be centuries from now, but I *will* take his place. The Medina-Jackyl line ends with me because I refuse to expose a woman to what I truly am. I'm a hybrid of demon and vampire, an anomaly, something that shouldn't exist, yet was prophe-sized. She doesn't think I know. In the future, my demon won't be easily hidden, the piece of me that's Jackyl will get pushed aside. It will push agonizingly to the surface and essentially take over. Feeding him will be the only way for me to exist."

"More than he did earlier?" Smiling sadly, she darted a look at Ripper to catch him shaking his head.

"That was playing around. I needed an advantage to tangle with my mother."

"You two did seem to be enjoying inflicting pain on each other."

"That was nothing, the last real fight we had was a century ago. She and I still have the scars from that one."

"I'm sure." Lifting her hand, she stroked Amora's cheek and watched her slightly stir. "Tell me how to make her stay."

"Unfortunately, I can't help you with that. Ma's made up her mind, and nothing is going to change that, but…" A mischievous tilt of his mouth appeared, and he grinned as he started backing out of the room. "I normally wouldn't suggest this, and it is particularly gag-worthy for me to even speak of it. Give my mother a reason to come home, if you know what I mean. I'm going for a run, probably be gone a few hours. You would have my undying appreciation if you were done by then."

She felt her face heat and her cheeks stung as she listened to him whistling as he left. Could she set aside her shyness? What if her journey into seduction was a disaster? Taking a deep breath, she lifted and straddled Amora's hips. Lowering her head, she flicked her tongue over a tightly furled nipple and then the other. Amora arched slightly, and steeling her nerve, Lark covered the peak of one breast, swirled her tongue around it and suckled. She bit down, and short nails abruptly seized her thighs. Repeating the motions on the other nipple and earned a deep rumbling moan.

Confidence grew at the sounds she provoked grew louder, and Amora shifted beneath her. So much power at her control, at least for now, she held no illusions that she would dominate long. But she would enjoy it while she could. Stroking her body over Amora's as she moved down the bed kissing scars, her tight nipples grazed Amora's skin and sent a shiver through her. She ached with a need for the pleasure she knew that only her mate could give her. She couldn't imagine allowing another to touch her.

She placed a small kiss beneath Amora's navel, leanly muscled legs parted as she nuzzled a small triangle of dark amber curls. They tickled her nose, and she placed small kisses to where thigh met groin, one side then the other. She savored the feel of silky flesh under her mouth, against her cheeks. The exact moment Amora fully awakened she knew, slender fingers combed through her hair and Lark froze. "Not going to stop now, are you? Tease."

Her eyes cast upward to catch a suggestive smirk and the flash of a tongue swirling around a fang. Wetness coated and trickled down her inner thighs at the gesture. She loved the feel of Amora's fangs on her skin. "I'm—I'm a bit nervous."

"You get control this once, baby, better make it good."

"Not helping, Amora." A sexy chuckle made her smile through her nervousness, and her tongue peeked out to trace Amora's slit. The vamp's hips arched and pressed closer to her mouth. Lark closed her eyes as she pushed her tongue into Amora's swollen lips and licked over the hard nub of her clit. Amora's nails dug into her scalp as the scent of her mate's arousal filled her nose and the taste burst on her tongue.

"Fuck, do that again." It was a growl and an order combined, she swirled her tongue and flicked. Lark repeated from memory the attention showed to her by Amora. Amora's hips jerked and fingers flexed to pull her deeper into the V of Amora's thighs. Closing her mouth around her mate's clit, she felt the subtle pulse upon her tongue as she sucked with gentle pressure. Her eyes opened to catch sight of Amora's upper body bowing upward. Slipping her right hand between her own thighs, she stroked her wet, sensitive lips, and delved between finding her aching bud.

Amora growled, and her head jerked back as she met slumberous black eyes. "No, don't touch, your pleasure is mine." She had no time to prepare before Amora turned her roughly onto her back. Amora's slender body rested heavy on hers. Amora nails scored, sharp teeth nipped and bit leaving her skin marked with red welts and light impressions of fangs.

Lark writhed and arched and struggled against Amora's superior strength to get closer. She cried out as fingers pinched her nipples roughly, plucked and tugged. Amora licked at her mouth, teasingly pulled away as she tried to capture her mate's lips.

"Amora, please, kiss me." She felt the smirk seconds before Amora thoroughly kissed her breathless. A desperate deep tongue thrusting melding of mouths. Her arms twined tightly around Amora's neck. Curled and teased her aching flesh as their bodies met in slow grinds.

"Are you ready for me to fuck you, my innocent Lark?"

"Wha-what do you—" Words stuttered to a stop as Amora surged upward and stared down at her. Her mate leaned to the side and opened the drawer on the bedside table. There was the rustling sound of plastic. She swallowed hard at the sight of leather and the thick outline of a penis. "You don't mean to…"

"Lark, every part of you belongs to me for as long as I say." Possessiveness laced words hitched her breathing in her chest until she grew dizzy. She watched with rapt attention to the securing of the harness. "I need this one memory, let me have it." Ripper's words came back to her; give her a reason to come home. She shivered as she nodded and observed as she opened a packet and slid a thin barrier over the shaft. "So sexy, innocent, I never—" She swore there were reverence and awe in her tone. Lark's mind went blank as Amora stroked her thumb over that sensitive bud hidden within her slit.

The vamp drew her short nails up Lark's right thigh as a gentle pressure urged Lark to lift her leg to rest her ankle on Amora's shoulder. Amora's fangs dragged over the inside of Lark's ankle.

"Just breathe, baby." She didn't understand until she felt the pressure begin, the unfamiliar intrusion. Lark gasped as the stretch became discomfort, but no pain. "Shh, love, relax. I will take such good care of my mate." Amora's slender hands firmly massaged her thighs as she steadily pulled her into Amora and her mate's hips thrust slow and easy.

"Amora, wait." Fear mixed with lust, the slight pain, but the hopeful expression on Amora's face made her war with herself. Sex wasn't like they'd described to her. She waited for the force and violence she'd been warned about, yet she only felt a slight twinge as she fully cradled Amora between her thighs. The feeling was odd, and not what she expected. She'd never expected— "Oh!" A backward stroke glided over rippling muscles and then returned in a shallow thrust.

"A good oh?" Lark didn't have time to think before the rhythm started slow and steady. Amora's thumb stroked over her nub. As her pace increased, Amora's eyes became heavier as they watched the bounce of Lark's breasts moving with each plunge. Strangeness became pleasure and she shook, and a high-pitched whimper took her unaware as Amora slid along that spot she'd only ever touched with her fingers. "That's my good girl."

Lark's head thrashing back and forth on the pillow, her fingers fisted in the sheets as she lifted. She rolled her hips to meet Amora's thrusts. The tightening in her lower belly, the tingle and ache of her nipples began the quick forming familiar orgasm. "Amora!" Panicked at the intensity, yet striving for more, but she couldn't reach it. The fall from the precipice the liberation of losing herself in the pleasure her mate gifted her.

Amora's body covered hers, her knee now rested on her mate's shoulder, and the thrusts increased to a sharp, shallow grind. "Come for me, let me taste it." A scream issued from between Lark's lips as fangs sunk brutally into the side of her throat and Amora's body arched as she drove into her quicker, the smooth leather rubbing against her clit. She clutched and clawed, heard the pleasured rumble as her body came apart. Her muscles clamped around the invasion of Amora's toy. Blank and lost, Lark was held in frightened suspension as ecstasy ripped through her.

The body atop hers trembled as fingers gripped her hair and Amora fed in great pulls on her throat. Lark held her breath, and her eyes rolled upward as her head began to float, thoughts hazy as her heart pounded sending blood roaring through her veins giving Amora what she needed. Tears stung her eyes, and she held tighter to Amora, she tried to hide the terror of losing her, but the whining growl coming from Amora proved she'd hid nothing.

Losing Amora wasn't an option, yet she knew that she would be left to await word if she'd lost the woman she had quickly come to love. Even if she could only enjoy the gift of Amora's possessiveness, it would be something she'd cherish. She wasn't the powerful vampire's mate, she was too weak and wouldn't be able to stand tall at Amora's side. For a few short weeks, the monster loved her into oblivion, and she'd have to hold onto the memories once Amora was gone and she was sent away to raise her sister alone.

CHAPTER 14

$\mathcal{A}$ majestic stone castle stood in the distance, Amora hid in the shadows as she observed the changing of shifts. She had hours of time ahead, yet too many scenarios of missteps and what-ifs plagued her mind. Lark sketched out the interior, giving her a route planned to get to Meadow and get her out. Leaving two days before had been harder than she thought, Lark's worried and sad expression tore had the heart she'd thought she'd lost long ago. A quick kiss, but she made no promises she'd be back.

Lying to Lark wasn't an option, she wouldn't give her mate false hope. Ripper had made quiet vows to take care of Lark. She had also made him promise not to come for her if they captured her. She went into this resigned to her fate, hoping upon hope it wasn't the trap she feared it was. She pushed up, it was now or never. Dressed entirely in black, she stuck to the shadows of the tree line and cool stone.

The old wooden door she was looking for came into view. Stopping in front of it, she checked for alarms and triggers for traps. Amora found none, so she put her shoulder to it and quickly broke the lock. The dungeon smelled moldy and musty. Terror tried to grip her as her mind tried to flash back. Amora growled and shook off the thoughts. Her mission at hand was the only thing that mattered.

Children were kept separately from their parents; bonds of family didn't exist. Your place predestined as Hunter or Breeder, an archaic caste system. They were taught their station and not to forget early. She heard footsteps and the murmurs of conversations from a distance. She smelled the thickness of adrenaline as bodies clashed. Sparring matches in the courtyard. She categorized, took mental note of every sound and smell.

Pausing outside a door, light bright around the edges and she listened, scented the air, but no one appeared to be near. Amora eased the door open, peeked out, checking left to right and left again. Reaching behind her, she slid her dagger from the sheath at the small of her back. It made a comforting whisper of sound, and she stepped out into the hall. She stayed to the side, and she twisted the blade to lay along her forearm.

On guard, observing with heightened senses as she hugged the walls mentally pulling up the schematic. A cry rang out from a distance and the alluring scent of fear washed in from all sides. She double-timed it, there was no time to waste, she had over-estimated her timeframe. It was only a matter of time before they discovered her. She had thought she'd have Meadow before her time ran out.

Bodies appeared from all sides as she reached a four-way junction, human bodies, frail and stinking of fear. She remembered the Hunters with more backbone. Although, you never took your opponent for granted. They would fight no fairer than she would. Steadying herself, lifting her arms in a defensive position—she wasn't a defenseless child held within chains. Amora had killed countless in battle, without remorse or mercy, tonight would be no different.

She would not succumb. Nostrils flared and weapons pulled, the group of men watched her with hate-filled gazes. Baring her fangs inside a thinned sneer of lips, she turned in a circle and waited for the first strike. They feigned attack, their arrogant posturing elicited no response. She would remain unbroken and the monster they feared in childish nightmares. They would die just like all the ones who came before.

A searing pain on her back caused a hiss as she spun on her toes striking the bulky male holding a red-tipped knife. Her arm arced cleanly through the air her blade slicing opening both cheeks as squeals widened her smile as he fell. The burning warmth of blood splashing across her face, and as she turned, her tongue flicked over her bloody lips.

The warmth rushed over her cool skin, the heady scent of death and the slow ebb of heartbeats faded. It sounded of victory, the more pain they inflicted, the harder she fought. The intoxicating rush of power, momentary highs of invincibility tempered by realism and still they fell around her. Wave after wave of bodies hyped up on testosterone and adrenaline and sprays of crimson touched her tongue, she tasted it all. Experienced it like a junkie's rush and she wanted more, that monster tearing to the surface.

The beast they created in the dungeon of a castle very much like this one. She straightened as she stepped over the carnage. Two flights of stairs, one right turn and then two left. They strived for dominance, to be her better, but she knew all their tricks. Ancestors before them trained her, she knew when to feign and when to charge. A beautifully, brutal choreographed dance nearly four centuries old and the slaughter made the immoral chasms of her soul burst with a savage violence. She'd hid this for so long, locked it away, although now it had built and this one last battle set it free.

A scent similar to her mate's found her senses as she crested the top of a staircase. She followed it to a closed door, then Amora pushed the door open and spotted Meadow. A miniature version of Lark, same dark waist-length tresses, and huge blue eyes stared at Amora with equal parts defiance and fear. She sheathed her knife in a fluid motion and approached the small girl. Amora refused to mask herself in shades of friendliness. Blood covered her from head to toe, without waiting she moved in a blur of motion across the room. She scooped the child into her arms. Meadow kicked and screamed, tiny nails tore at the tender skin of Amora's face.

"Lark may want you, but I'll leave your little ass, do we understand each other?" She growled the words, but the struggles ceased as soon as she'd mentioned Lark.

"Lark?" Meadow's gaze turned teary as two perfect drops spilled over her bottom lashes. The quick acquiescence prickled uneasily at her nape, but she sensed no deception. Just the learned skill of bowing to an Alpha.

"She sent me for you. Hold on, be quiet. And whatever you do, don't scream." Waves bounced around the cherub face, and she seemed to pull into herself. All childish fear disappeared. The shift surprised her, there was nothing of Lark's openness in the child in her arms.

She heard them coming in the heaviness of footsteps and shouts for backup. Amateurs, how far the fearsome Order had fallen since they last clashed. Small, chubby arms and legs circled her neck and waist. Drawing her weapon as she stepped into the hall, she wouldn't use the child as a shield, but she wouldn't put Meadow at her back where she couldn't hold tight to her.

Bodies filled each end of the hall, a phalanx she'd have to tear through. "Honey, close your eyes and don't open them until I tell you to." She darted a look down in time to see eyes squeezing shut.

One-armed and at a disadvantage, she stepped forward three steps and stood in the middle of the large hallway. The windows of Meadow's room were only large enough for a child to squeeze through. Her only option was to fight like hell and hope she could protect Meadow in the process. Amora closed her eyes, behind her lids a picture of her mate formed. Smiling plump lips and loving eyes, the day Lark had protected her from Ripper, and the first time she'd seen her mate's face flushed with pleasure. She closed her eyes tighter as she remembered the first time she'd tasted love.

If it was her night to die, she'd accept it, but she wouldn't go down without fighting for one more chance to feel peace and taste love flowing over her tongue.

Amora opened her eyes, a cold smirk tilted the corners of her mouth and she panned from one end of the hall to the other. She deftly flipped the knife until the cold steel lay comfortingly along the back of her forearm, and she steeled herself for the first wave. They came for her with a grand battle cry, and she turned as the first one reached. He struck with no thoughts of the child. He drew first blood with a searing plunge of his blade through her forearm. Flesh and muscle gave as she ripped her arm from the weapon while driving hers into his throat.

They howled with discovery as they aimed each time for the child and she spun taking their hits—the pummeling of blades. The hilt slipped from her useless hand as she wrapped herself around Meadow, listened to the low whimpers as she cried and Amora hugged her tighter. She fell shielding Meadow cocooned in the shelter of her body. Heavy boots connected with her back as she pulled Meadow's arms and legs beneath her.

She felt the moment her body had enough in the blackening of her vision, the fading of the pain and somewhere on the outskirts of her consciousness she heard the order to cease. "Tell Lark I'm sorry." She groaned the words as she was dragged away from the muffled cries of a child slowly fading. Where they would take her was no secret, she knew what was to befall her. Once more she would pray to the God she cursed centuries before, she would beg that same God to let her die.

CHAPTER 15

"No! Stop, please, you're killing her." Lark fought the steely grip of restraining hands. The tears streamed down Meadow's cheeks as Amora took every blow. Pain ripped through her stomach, across her back as she tried to throw herself on Amora. Strong arms circled her waist, words muffled in her ear as she clawed to get to Meadow and Amora. Gaze darting down to see seeping crimson wounds and confusion took over.

Childish cries as tears flowed from squeezed eyes. Amora protected Meadow, put her body on the line and took it. Kicks that echoed with the sickening sounds of bones cracking and she only held tighter to Meadow. Wetness felt hot on her cool skin, she felt everything her mate felt. Rage seethed as she reached for Amora's fallen blade. It was a consuming thirst to kill, revulsion and anger warred for dominance. Undertones of fear buried deep beneath the compulsion to fight, survive and protect. Her arm swung through the air, blindly lashing out.

"Lark! Wake the fuck up!" The force of the hand across her cheek forced her eyes open as her head swam.

"Wha-what's…I have to get to them!"

"What did you see? Lark?" Ripper shook her as he watched her with unnerved expression in his green eyes. "Focus, what did you see?"

"They kept kicking, the blades kept slicing flesh, and she let them. Why would she, she's supposed to fight..." Her words stuttered amid sobs as she clung to Ripper.

"Did she have Meadow?"

"Sheltered beneath her, but she was scared, wouldn't open her eyes, just kept crying, I tried to get to them, I swear I did."

"She put herself on the line for your sister, are you happy now? I should have put a stop—" A loud hiss and the strange whisper of a rattle caused her to flinch as she saw the rippling of shimmering black scaly skin covered most of Ripper's partially exposed body.

"It was, Ripper, it was just a dream."

"You're my mother's mate, the bond isn't strong like it should be, but it's there. Fuck!" His fist connected shaking the support pillar as he paced.

"I'm not her mate, she would've told me."

"No, she wouldn't have. Innocence and beauty have no business belonging to something like Amora."

Lark was still lost in the dream—or was it a vision? Amora had done that for Meadow, for her, she buried her face in her hands as she wept. The worst of her nightmares came true, Amora wouldn't come back to her.

"We're going after them."

"Amora said—" She pressed back against the wall as Ripper was there, his face inches from hers with needle-like fangs dripping venom.

"I don't give a fuck what Amora said, I won't let her die in a dungeon, or worse go mad as some fucked-up cult's weapon and toy." He jerked away, and she tore at the hem of her gown as she felt the drops of poison burn through cotton to flesh. "Get your shit together, we have to get to Seamus', we'll need an army. Nothing of that fucking place will be left standing when I'm through if she's dead."

* * *

THE TEA she sipped did nothing to alleviate nausea caused by Ripper's flashing thing. Rumbles of outrage traveled around camp. The Alpha seethed as his muscles rippled somewhere in the tenuous space between human and animal. An army, a rescue party, formed within moments of their arrival. Each one was willing to lay their lives on the line for Amora Medina-Jackyl and all for reasons surprising and familiar causing Lark's eyes to burn with the need to cry.

A mate saved, a child cared for or a tender touch in grief. Amora was more than she let the collective see. Was it to make up for the blood she swore she owed for? All the lives she'd taken in the name of revenge?

"Kali will sense your presence as soon as you dematerialize, Ripper. You know he watches you and keeps track. We have to do this the old-fashioned way. Lark knows the layout, we make a plan and strike. Amora is our objective." Seamus cast his wife a soft look and Lark looked away from the intimacy in the shared moment.

"We can't wait! She may already be—" She watched as Seamus' arm shot out and a huge hand wrapped around Ripper's nape. Ripper was pulled forward until their foreheads rested together.

"If she's dead, then no one remains standing. We get her out, that's our only objective." Something moved between the two men, a son's respect for his father, not merely a pack member's respect for their Alpha. "Amora deserves her retribution, let your mother alone have that honor, Son."

"Seamus, I can't lose her, she's all I have."

Lark bit her lip as she watched the tough son of her mate crumbled and cry. Not great heaving sobs, but a silent suffering. A jerk of Seamus' head cleared the tent.

"We'll get her back, dead or alive, we bring her home." The Alpha's voice boomed, a vow Lark felt Seamus would die to keep.

"Lark, do you feel her?" Yvette knelt carefully in front of her, and she met kind eyes, Lark's semi-calm breaking as soft, yet strong hands cupped her cheeks. "In your heart and soul, do you feel your mate?"

"I thought it was just a dream, a nightmare and she'd be home."

"Close your eyes, is she alive? Lark, does Amora still exist?" Lark closed her eyes and took a deep breath, letting it out slowly. The pain and rage were muted, although still there, Lark felt a sense of failure and a longing for something. What that something was seemed concealed beneath cloying layers of camouflage.

"Yes, she's still alive, I can feel it. Why do I feel like she's in my head and I'm in hers?"

"I don't understand why Amora didn't tell you. Some part of her has secretly longed for love, peace and ultimate understanding. Sometimes we bond with our mates on a level so deep that our soul is consumed by theirs as much as ours is consumed by theirs. Amora lives, it's not an intense bond, the claiming wasn't complete. She left you your humanity and the fickleness of mortality. It was her kindness in the face of you losing her. Our Amora cares deeply for you." She furrowed her brow at Yvette's small smile. "To be loved by Amora must mean you bring her soul the peace she's craved for so many centuries."

"Why wouldn't she tell me?" Her lip quivered as she asked and received a sympathetic look.

"Would you lay your soul bare for another when you can make no promises of forever with them? She knew, in some part of her, she would not return. Amora also knew her son would no more heed her order than she would his in the same circumstance." Lark dropped her eyes to her lap and wrung her hands. "One way or another, she would give you your precious sister. Honor the gift Amora gave you, she fought for what was yours, now you do the same, you fight for her. You go to war, stand in battle back to back with your family. For your family." Lark nodded as Yvette called Seamus over to assist her to her feet. He chuckled as he nuzzled his mate's neck and rubbed the roundness of her belly.

"Lark, you'll come with us, Amora will need you when we rescue her. Although, be prepared to mourn rather than celebrate the return of your mate. The female who left us is more than likely not returning, the monster may very well be."

Lark nodded again, at a loss for what to say, the shame and guilt choked her. If only she had returned, but her selfishness caused all this. Left alone with her thoughts as Seamus led Yvette away and Ripper exited the tent without glancing at her. She had ruined lives, brought this on them, how many would die to repair her mistake? Lifting her hand, Lark gently touched the fading marks hidden by the sweep of her long hair. Could she face the consequences? Amora had tried to teach her that first night about penalties for her decisions. She just wished she had learned it before now.

CHAPTER 16

*B*ars instead of tattered curtains covered the thin, rectangular slit of a window. It was only wide enough to let in the cool breeze. Hours, days, maybe weeks had passed, time didn't tick away as it should. Time measured in punches, burns and the thirst. Bare and bloody, raw as an exposed nerve, pale flesh marred by the split skin of whip marks. Amora could barely lift her head, yet when they came for her, she was a warrior, strong and unmerciful.

History was repeating harshly; they drained her at regular intervals. The hunger consumed her, tore at her gut. She wouldn't allow them to see her weak, nor would she beg. Soon the heavy footfalls of boots would approach, and it would all begin again.

Her shoulders ached from the pull of her weight, and her joints were close to dislocation. Legs too weak to bear her weight, yet when the time came she would stand proud. The arrival of the sunrise an uncomfortable sensation under her skin, with cruel certainty she knew today it would happen.

Lashes fluttered closed as she pulled up memories, remembrances she never allowed herself to have. Loving kisses to her scars, a gift of innocence that a monster like she should never have been allowed to touch. The feel of Lark tucked trustingly against her side. A momentary, yet an overwhelming sense of peace, days of nightmares pushed away by the love she'd so fleetingly tasted. Unworthy, stained with so many years of maliciousness, and still somehow, she was deemed valuable enough to be bestowed with affection and devotion. She held those memories close as she forced herself to her feet as the grind of the old iron lock sounded through the room.

Sneering at the men who entered the room, she prepared, she would take it, and Amora would howl in victory through the pain as she didn't break.

* * *

"Fuck you!" Amora laughed hysterically and only faltered long enough to spit in the bastard's face. A full five days of torture behind her and she was positive there were many more to come.

Arms flexed and pulled at the shackles at her wrists, the paper-thin starved flesh stripped away by layers. She accepted it, welcomed it and used it to fuel the rage and insanity. "Again." The glowing orange branding iron connected with brutal force against her abdomen. She hissed and mocked, at the stench of burned flesh, but this pain was nothing compared to what awaited. The inevitability of her death was a simple reality Amora would embrace when it finally came.

"Let's see how tough you are when your precious sun is licking over your flesh." Her smile nearly faded at the huge man's words. Amora's gaze skittered to the pale rays filtering through the window.

"Been there, done that, motherfucker, you've got to do better," she taunted them even as her body grew weaker. The feel of the restraints easing around her wrists and ankles caused a mixture of relief and panic.

Amora straightened her shoulders as two other men gripped her arms and led her from her cell. Stumbling once, twice, to their amusement and bellowed chuckles. Anger grew at her show of weakness. Paraded through a gauntlet of bodies, old, young, male, female, she kept her gaze forward.

They showed her off as a freak in a sideshow, to demonstrate their superiority to the creature who haunted their nights. A flash of movement at the corner of her eye caught her attention, and she saw Meadow. She jerked at the restraining hands as rage burned through her at the bruise upon the chubby cheek.

"This isn't such a good day to die after all." Her lips pulled into a smirk. "Let's see how you like the real monster." With the last reserves of strength, she spun her head and fangs sank into the meaty thickness of one of the guard's throats. She covered his body as she took him to the ground, with great pulls she fed as high-pitched screams and deep bellows rang out somewhere in the distance.

Hands tried to pull her away, but she drank her fill until she was ripped away from his throat. She surged to her feet as she spat the hunk of flesh to the stone floor. Crouching low she took the blade from the sheath on the male's belt, flipped and measured its weight. Amora tilted her head as she spotted Meadow in the same spot with her eyes squeezed shut and she closed the distance between them and knelt.

"Meadow, run, hide, I'll come for you when it's safe." The child hesitated. "Go!" That one word and tiny pink sneakers pounded against the floor. A flash of the night her parents and siblings died came unbidden to her mind. She had told Bram she would come for them too. Rage poured through her, vengeance was hers. Once more she would stand and watch everything burn. But when she finished this time, she would make sure no one remained.

Chaos reigned as she watched it all in slow motion, the thunderous sound of a single gunshot and she turned avoiding it. Tossing the knife up, she caught the cool tip between her fingers and sent it sailing through the air. She moved with blurring motions and pulled the blade from the shooter's throat. A twisted amusement made her chuckle at his gurgling as he pressed the wound with futility.

They arrived in waves, blade and gun, burning hot bullets buried themselves in her body and the sting of blades plunging or slicing. It mattered not, they fell, and she fought through the gauntlet of Hunters. With every one that fell, the demon of her past pushed to the surface, drove away all lingering humanity. Executioner, a vessel for the vengeance of immeasurable lives taken in the name of false gods and idols and she was invincible.

A hand landed on her shoulder, and she pivoted on her toes, blade stopping at the tender column of a throat. "Ripper, what the fuck did I tell you?"

"Yeah, I kinda said fuck it and called in backup." Amora shot a look over her son's shoulder, and Seamus and Fernando appeared around the corner.

"We'll talk about this later."

"Ma, can't you just let yourself be rescued every once in a while? I was looking forward to bragging rights."

"Fuck you, give me your shirt." Ripper lifted his t-shirt over his head, and Amora quickly pulled it over her head. "Did you bring my babies?" She smiled as Ripper handed her the holster with her blades. "You're good for something."

"Kali is sending backup, someone sent word. We have to go."

"Not until this is finished."

"We'll come back, let's go."

"I have to get Meadow. Where's the meet-up point?"

"South wall of the courtyard, but I'm going with you."

"Fine, try to keep up." She closed her eyes, focused on Meadow's scent beneath the stench of blood and terror. Corridors and opened doors flew by as Ripper remained on her heels. They fought back to back, adrenaline surged as Hunters fell one after another.

She stopped as Meadow's scent became stronger, dripped with terror and pain. Growling she threw her weight against a door, and it splintered open. A man well over six feet, held Meadow to his chest as she kicked and clawed. He clutched the little girl's throat, and Meadow gasped in pain. "The great Amora Jackyl, the fiercest weapon The Order ever possessed. You're weak to care about a mere child. Am I safe in assuming you came for her because the Breeder sent you?"

"Are you going to hide behind her?" She started to step forward when the sound of fabric billowing preceded the bright morning sun shining across the library.

"Not so tough now."

"I'm plenty tough." She turned and looked at Ripper. "When he drops her, grab her and go, don't look back."

"Let me take him."

"Do as I say." Facing forward as she calculated her plan, the smirk returning to her mouth and she met Meadow's eyes. "Remember what I told you." The tiny replica of her mate nodded and eyes closed as Amora struck. She smelled the stench of burned flesh, felt the searing pain, but she didn't slow. She attacked with fists and weapon as she forced him back into the shadows of the stacks. She listened to the shuffle of feet and Ripper speaking comfortingly to Meadow.

Amora pushed through the agony, savored it and used it to make her brawl harder. Vicious and unstoppable, he made his moves, took his shots, but they did nothing. She slammed his burly body against the wall, lifted him and pinned him there with blades through each shoulder. He screamed as she released his weight and the sharp edges caught on bone.

"My mate told me about you. You like to use your size against defenseless women."

"Mate?" He spat out the question through his pain.

"Lark." The male's eyes widened to her mirth. "I have to leave, as you can see." She motioned to the blistered and blackened flesh. "I don't do well in the sun for long, but let your precious Kali know I *will* be back, I *will* destroy you all with a smile on my face." She wrapped her hands around the hilts and pulled so he fell in a heap at her feet.

Sheathing her weapons, she eyed a thick tapestry and ripped it from its hanger. Amora wrapped it around herself until no skin remained uncovered. It wouldn't help for long in direct sunlight, but it was something until she made it out. Regret at leaving the place standing tore at her, but getting Meadow safe and getting back to her mate was more important. Tearing The Order down to its last brick would come soon enough.

CHAPTER 17

*L*ark paced the length of the small cabin. She couldn't tell if it was night or day as all the windows were blacked out. They had left hours ago, her skin crawled with emotions not her own. She held onto hope it meant Amora was still alive. The worry for Amora and Meadow tore her apart. If it was daytime, they couldn't bring Amora home. Would she have to wait hours more for word? Tires on gravel alerted her to someone coming, she reached for the gun Seamus left with her. Lark wrapped her fingers around the grip, her index finger poised over the trigger guard. The weight was heavy and unfamiliar as she moved until her back met the cabin wall.

Breathing slow and easy, Lark tried to calm her heart. Had they found her? Were her mate and the others captured? The worst-case scenarios spun in dizzying circles in her head. She jumped as the door flew open and a cloaked figure pushed inside.

"Baby, you're not going to shoot me, are you?" Relief nearly took her legs from beneath her, and she ran across the room throwing herself into Amora's arms. Heedless of the blood and wounds that covered Amora, she just held tight and kissed cheeks, eyes and lips. Tears streamed down her face.

"I thought you were gone, oh, I couldn't—" Amora's tongue pushed roughly passed her lips and took her breath. Losing herself in the melding of mouth and stroking of tongues, she moaned as hands forced their way beneath her skirt. Strong hands molded the cheeks of her bottom.

A throat cleared. "Um, a child present, innocent eyes." With a chuckle, Amora broke the kiss and set her on her feet. Her mate stepped aside, and Lark sagged, falling to her knees at the beautiful face smiling at her.

"Lark!" Her arms reached out as the tiny, solid body slammed into her and she hugged her sister tight. Sobbing as she buried her face in Meadow's soft hair that smelled of baby powder.

"Oh, baby, are you okay?" She retreated, wildly searched her baby sister for injury between hugs and kisses. The dark bruise on Meadow's face broke her heart. She gently stroked her fingertips over it and then wept louder.

"She's okay." Amora appeared at her side, arms wrapped around her waist and cool lips brushed her cheeks.

"'Mora said she was bringing me to you. I was good, I listened." A small smile curved her lips as she watched her baby sister pantomime Amora saving her.

"I think she's talking me up a bit, I didn't do that flipping kick thing." Lark jerked her gaze to Amora as the woman stood and pushed the heavy covering off her shoulders. Her hands flew to her mouth covering the cry at the numerous wounds—the burns that had yet to begin healing.

"Amora?" Once again guilt assailed her as she took in the damage.

"Her and you were worth it, don't think anything else. Is the bathroom vamp-proofed?" Lark couldn't speak past the lump in her throat, so she merely nodded. "Spend time with Meadow, I need to get cleaned up and then I have more work to do." Amora walked off after tweaking a wave of Meadow's hair and winking at the little girl.

"Don't, let her have some time." Seamus knelt beside them and grinned broadly at Meadow, the little girl batted her lashes. "A flirt, Amora will have her hands busy one day when the boys start sniffing. She's brave, she tried to take on Amora, I hear."

"Did you?" She arched her brow at Meadow, and her sister dropped her eyes to the toes of her sneakers.

"I fought, just as they told me." The words were years older than the four-year-old who stood in front of her.

"Is Amora okay?"

"She had taken out quite a few Hunters before we arrived. We should have known she wouldn't be one to wait simply for a rescue. I don't know how okay she is. We don't know what they did to her before she was able to free herself. Spend some time with Meadow. Amora will need you shortly, but not yet." Lark nodded as she wrapped her arms around Meadow and lifted the small body as she stood. Carrying her to the kitchen, finding a rag and cleaning her dirty face. She made Meadow something to eat, sure the little girl was hungry. Lark handed Meadow the sandwich and watched her take tiny bites.

Her sister kept darting her gaze around the room, almost as if she didn't believe it was real.

"I told you I would find a way to get you." Curious eyes watched her as Meadow chewed nervously on her bottom lip. "What's wrong, Meadow?"

"Why were you kissing a girl?"

"Well, um…" Lark knew what they taught the followers and she knew what she felt, but how do you explain loving someone when love and affection were considered weak traits? She couldn't use the example of a loving mom and dad. Breeding was for procreation only. Love wasn't involved, Lark tried to find an explanation.

Fingers pulled her hair back, and soft lips dropped a kiss to the side of her throat. Amora's slender body moved in tight behind her and twined arms around her waist.

"She was kissing me because she loves me."

"But only girls and boys can make babies."

"Loving someone doesn't have anything to do with making babies. She's my mate, my heart." Lark jerked in Amora's arms and stopped breathing. Amora was hers, the revelation made her wobbly and only her mate's embrace kept her on her feet. "So, get used to me kissing your sister, or you can go live with Ripper."

"Hey, don't pawn the munchkin off on me, you two can control your nasty urges, but…" Ripper swooped in and swung Meadow off the counter. "I always wanted a sister. I can teach her how to annoy you. Come with me, I have secrets and lessons to share to torture your Momma Amora."

"Be nice, or I'll disown your ass." Amora playfully growled as Ripper snorted, Lark turned to cast a glance over her shoulder at her mate.

"Yes, Mommy Dearest. We don't listen to her, Meadow, she's all growl and no bite. A softie, let me tell you." A small smile pulled at the corners of her mouth as Amora rolled her eyes and shook her head.

Pressure on her hips urged her to turn, and when she did, she kept her gaze on Amora's upper chest. "Look at me." She slowly raised her eyes.

"I didn't think you were coming back. Why weren't you honest with me?"

"Lark, I couldn't make promises. I knew if I didn't make it back, Ripper would get Meadow for you." Lark threw her arms around Amora and held tight.

"Thank you for Meadow, but why wouldn't you tell me before how you felt?"

"Baby, you've been around me long enough, I am as allergic to feelings as a man."

"Be serious, no jokes or sarcasm." She demanded an honest answer, not one cloaked in diversion.

"If I didn't come back, you could move on, find another, I made sure that you would be well provided for if I died."

"I don't care about your damn money. I wanted you, just you, to stay." Cool, slender hands cupped her cheeks, and thumbs stroked along her wet lashes.

"Do you know how many I have killed? Not over my many years, but in the last days, I have vowed to destroy, to make sure no one lives to create another generation of Hunters. I enjoyed the taking of their lives. Can you spend the rest of your life or the eternity I may give you with a monstrosity, a mistake of nature?"

"Yes, because you are more than that. Seamus' pack jumped at the chance to rescue you. You protected a child that you have no bond with, I saw and felt it." Lark fisted her hands in Amora's shirt and shut her eyes to hold back the tears. "They tried to kill her, and you took every blow knowing they would discover you would put yourself on the line to save her. A monster doesn't do that. I don't think I would love a monster." Lark whispered the last sentence as she laid her forehead on Amora chest, her mate dropped a kiss to her hair.

"Lark, don't see more than what's there. I have very few regrets in this life. Failing my parents in my inability to save my siblings, is one of them. I promised them I'd come back for them and instead, they burned. I sold my soul for revenge, lived and existed for it, that won't change. When I'm completely ready, I'll go back, and no one will remain alive."

"You do what you have to, but it won't change that I *will still* wait."

"We'll see, Lark." Gentle pressure on her chin lifted her head, and Amora kissed her softly. "Tonight, we go home, until then, sleep with me."

She nodded her head as she slipped from between Amora and the counter. Taking her mate's hand, she led her to the bedroom they'd prepared for Amora. The knowledge this wasn't over, there still awaited another strike caused a tear to slip from the corner of her eye. Another wait on her part as her mate did what needed to be done.

She wrapped herself around Amora as they lay on the lumpy mattress, placed her head on Amora's chest and listened to the nearly non-existent beat. Just a sound for show. Fingers combed gently through her hair as she closed her eyes. What-ifs and scenarios best left alone, not thought of, but she couldn't just *not* think. Tightening her arms around Amora, embracing her firmly with some naïve hope that the closer she kept her mate, the longer she would be allowed to have her.

CHAPTER 18

Steam filled the bathroom as Amora closed the door quietly behind her and leaned against it. She watched Lark through the hazy, glass shower walls with a smirk. They had arrived back in New Orleans only hours before, and she'd settled Meadow in the living room with new toys. When Amora pushed her shoulders away from the door, she began to strip slowly while she strode across the room. She opened the door, she stepped inside and slipped her arms around Lark's waist.

"Hey, baby." She wrapped the heavy, wet mass of Lark's hair around her fist and lifted it to press her face into the curve of her mate's neck.

"What are you doing? Meadow…" She shut Lark up with a gentle tug and sharp nip at the warm skin.

"She's occupied." Stroking her palms upward over the curve of Lark's belly to cup the fullness of her breasts and teased her fingertips over hard nipples. Lark trembled as she repeated the caress. Amora spun them, she wrapped her fingers around Lark's wrists and placed them on the tiled wall above her head. "Leave them there." Amora splayed her left hand on her mate's stomach flexed and pulled Lark

119

back until she bent slightly at the waist. She smoothed her hands over the wet curves of Lark's ass, squeezed and parted the curves.

Her name was a breathless whimper, and she loved the sound of it tipping over Lark's plump lips. She smacked one cheek, then the other repeatedly until Lark arched her back into each slap. Sweet shampoo and arousal filled the steamy interior. She praised, soothed and repeated the sharp strikes. "So sexy when you beg me."

Roughly, she gripped Lark's hair and turned her until she could take her lips in a brutal, passionate kiss. She rubbed the cradle of her hips to the hot, reddened curves and drank in her lover's moan. Her free hand glided over curves, tracing the valleys and hills of Lark's small, curvy form. Helpless in her craving to possess, mark every inch as hers. Tracing the tip of her tongue along the sharp edge of Lark's teeth, she was learned the silkier texture of the underside of her tongue.

She growled as she pulled away and dropped to her knees behind Lark. Amora palmed the plump cheeks as she leaned in stroking her cheeks over the softness of skin. She inhaled the musk of Lark's need, then with a broad, slow stroke of her tongue, licked along her pretty slit. She plunged and curled her tongue as she entered the clenched entrance of Lark's pussy. Lark let out a squeal of surprise, and she grinned as she flicked over her in lightning-fast flicks. The voluptuous body jerked and pushed back, hiked her hips higher opening her farther to Amora's questing tongue.

"Lark! What wrong? Why's door locked?" Amora growled at Meadow's concerned voice.

"Meadow, go play, I am just helping Lark wash her hair."

"She's not going away." There was amusement in Lark's voice, and she punished her with another smack.

"I know you're not finding this funny."

"No, love, never."

"Uh huh." The door rattled, and tiny fists beat on it.

"Let me in," Meadow demanded.

"Meadow, you want to play hide and seek?" She bit Lark's hip as the woman outright laughed.

"Really?"

"Yeah, hide and I'll come and find you. I bet I can't."

"Okay!" A high-pitched giggle that bordered on maniacal carried through the door as bare feet pounded on hardwood floors.

"That was mean." Amusement and admonishment warred in her mate's voice.

"It worked. Now, where were we? Oh, yes!" Lark batted her away, and she shot her mate an arched browed glare.

"We can't, she knows you're in here." Amora dropped her head in defeat.

"Is it too late to put my new kid up for adoption?"

"Yes, it is." Amora sank her fangs into one ample cheek and growled before pulling away and pushing to her feet.

"You have a cruel streak, and I don't appreciate it." She tried to hide her smile as Lark turned to look up at her with twinkling eyes.

"You love it, and you know it."

"No, I don't." Amora slapped Lark's ass as she stepped out of the shower. "I have a kid to find, would serve her right if I let her stay hidden until she got hungry or bored."

"Be nice and play."

"Uh huh, I might have a snack, so, if we're missing a kid…"

Her woman cackled, a real-life mean-spirited cackle then peeked around the shower door. "Stop! There better be a mini-terror found before I get out of the shower."

Amora dried off and dressed watching her mate a little longer.

"Yeah, yeah, I make no guarantees." Amora closed the bathroom door behind her and stepped out into the main room. She shook her head with a roll of her eyes at the tiny toes stuck out from underneath a thick tapestry covering one of the large windows. Amora shrugged and headed for the kitchen, the kid was on her own. Opening the fridge and pulling out a blood bag, she poured a mug and placed it on the warmer as her phone rang. "Yeah?"

"No wonder I have no manners to speak of." Ripper's voice made her growl.

"What do you want?"

"Can we meet up? I have something I need to talk to you about."

"Why not, see you in a second." As soon as she disconnected the call, Ripper materialized across from her. "If this is going to fuck up my day be prepared to die."

"Um…" Amora groaned as her son backed up putting space between them. "After your little carnage fest at the castle, I got nosy and snuck back in."

"What the fuck? Are you out of your mind?"

"Take a fucking downer, Ma, this isn't just your life on the line. You ever think about my fucked-up future."

"'Mora, he said bad word." She groaned as a little hand tugged at her shirt.

"I thought I told you to hide until I found you."

"I got hungry. Snack, please."

"Fine." She grabbed an apple and a knife, deftly peeling it before handing it to Meadow. "Now, go play." She shot her son a glare as he snickered. "Don't start."

"You're cute with a kid."

"I'm debating whether adoption is an option. She's coochie blocking me with my mate."

"Finally finding a set and admitting it, huh?" Ripper asked.

"Laugh and see what happens." Amora pointed at him with the tip of the blade, and the fucker snickered again. "What's this news?"

"Nicolette might be alive."

The world ceased as it felt like she took a sledgehammer to the gut and the knife fell from her limp fingers. She braced her hands palm down on the counter.

"Ma, talk to me." Ripper's voice muffled as she pictured the tiny heart-shaped face of Nicolette, the silky black waves that hung to her shoulders.

"Where?" Her voice was a menacing growl as she felt her eyes change and looked at her son with sharpened vision.

"I don't know. Lark mentioned a section of the library that was forbidden. When I went, I found a book, practically disintegrating and the writing was barely legible. There were a few notes about Medina-

Jackyl offspring. Naomi deceased, but Nicolette survived. Some of the notes mentioned missions to finish their job, but the Pure-born disappeared about two-hundred years ago. No notes after that."

"What about Bram?"

"I don't know."

"We go back."

"No, I'll go back, but you're staying away. Fuckers want your ass dead, no more weapon talk, Kali wants your head on a platter."

"That's nothing fucking new. If Nico's is alive, I'm going to fucking find her. Family doesn't get left behind, and I have a score to settle."

"You've done enough dam—" Her fist slammed down on the counter, and the butcher block creaked under the force.

"Until they are all dead, I have done nowhere near enough damage. I go back. Meadow's safe here with Lark. If you're not going to be my backup, you can get the fuck out of my way. Son or not, you don't want to tangle with me."

"We'll go, but I don't fucking like it. What about Seamus or Fernando, we could use another set of eyes. Do you think Lark knows something? Maybe something she's read but didn't pay attention to."

"She's in the shower. If Nico's still alive, we don't stop looking until we find her, understood?" Ripper nodded with an intense look in his eyes she was sure matched her own.

Nicolette alive, could that mean that the others survived? Amora dropped her chin to her chest, so many years lost. Watching their home burn, she'd never even dreamed her siblings survived. She wouldn't stop until she knew for sure. The Order had sins beyond her torture and the murder of her parents to answer for, and she would wring it from them by any means necessary.

CHAPTER 19

*P*layful Amora had disappeared by the time Lark stepped out of the shower. The intense wild look in her mate's eyes tightened her stomach with fear. She linked and twisted her fingers as she dropped her chin. Her hair concealed her face as she waited for the blow-up.

"Did you know my sister was possibly alive?" The coldness in Amora's tone made her flinch, yet her head popped up with eyes full.

"No, if I had known, I would have told you." Her voice lifted with a hysterical edge.

"Ripper." Amora motioned to Ripper with a tip of her head drawing Lark's attention to the man standing behind and to the left of her mate. "Found some journal entries in a book in the forbidden section of your library."

"I rarely ventured into that section, the few times I did, I only read accounts of your time in captivity and later entries of sightings of you."

"Lark, you have a photographic memory, do you remember anything at all? I don't care how small the details." Amora approached her, wrapped her in strong arms and pulled her flush against her body.

125

"I swear the only mention of your siblings were sections about their death the night your parents died. If I'd known your sister or the others were alive, I would have told you right away. As far as I knew The Order believed the other Medina-Jackyl offspring to be dead. It was a disappointment, and they cursed their nearsighted beliefs. They had plans for all the children. What would be better than one weapon was four conditioned to kill at The Order's whim? Stronger than hundreds of trained Hunters combined."

"Who would have been charged with all the records?"

"Dominic, he's the oldest of our Elders, well-protected. He carries the job of passing down the oral history of The Order to the next in line. Rumors are he's ancient, Kali appointed Dominic himself. If anyone knows all the dirty secrets, then it would be him. No one knows where to find him though. His location is kept a secret by the Elder Council."

"Then we kill the Elders one by one until they tell us what we need to know."

"You can't go back, Amora, there's no reason." She cried out as Amora roughly ripped herself from Lark's arms.

"There are three excellent reasons! They could all have survived. I won't stop until I find them and will do whatever needs to be done to determine if they are dead or alive." Her mate's voice was the coldest she'd ever heard it, and her heart broke as the woman turned away from her to storm off. Rage and sadness swamped her as Amora's emotions filled her, driving out even Lark's own emotions.

Hours had passed, and Amora hadn't returned yet. Ripper watched her with kind eyes as she paced. He tended to Meadow when needed and even put the child to bed. "I feel as if I'm losing her."

"Going from believing you lost your whole family to the possibility of them, even a few of them, being alive is like the most secret dream come true. You just need to let her work out the anger and hurt, she'll be back soon and be her usual self."

"Does she believe that I would keep something so important to her secret?" Her voice broke with tears she fought to keep hidden.

"No, I should have been a little more delicate than just blurting out

Nicolette may be alive. Although, I never learned tact or diplomacy, you know who my mother is."

Lark hugged her arms to her stomach as she slowly strode to the tapestry-covered window and with one hand slid it open to expose the starry night sky. She rubbed her right hand over her arm as she leaned against the window frame. It seemed colder than it should be and with a frightening clarity, she understood that when Amora returned, it would only be to say goodbye again. Lark would wait, she didn't have any another option. The constant fear of losing her mate wouldn't become any easier, yet she hoped one day she wouldn't have to worry about it.

"Don't look for heartache where there is none. She'll leave, but she'll come back. Amora loves you, I don't know if she's come out and said it yet, but I know she does. My mother wouldn't have laid her life on the line for your sister if she didn't. She may not even understand what it is, mates bond, but I don't believe it's all that insta-love bullshit."

"I guess I was just naïve in thinking that I wouldn't have to remain behind. Part of me wants her to find all her siblings alive, to once again have her family. Although a selfish part wants to hold on and somehow make her forget." She felt shame in admitting that, how cruel a person was she if she wished that Amora would only forget about her family. Lark endangered her mate when she'd asked for help to rescue Meadow, and Amora nearly sacrificed her life to make her happy. How could she expect any different when it came to Amora's sisters and brother?

"Not selfish, Lark, I would prefer her not go either. I would try to talk her out of it if I could. If what I found out is true, there's hope Nicolette and the rest are alive. I can't ask her to forget that."

"Will you be going with her? She won't be going alone. I need someone there to watch her, to keep her safe for me." She relaxed slightly when Ripper merely nodded and leaned opposite her. If her mate didn't survive, would she feel it as strongly as Amora's pain or rage? Lark didn't know if she wanted to know or if it would be kinder to wait for the distressing news.

"Do you know you give away your emotions quickly?"

"It's one of the reasons I failed as a Hunter."

"How does that work?"

"Your training begins at the age of four or five, at the age of two they separate you from your parents. Kept in the nursery wing for observation and I was easily frightened. They had high expectations for me since I was born of two Hunters. Soon their disappointment grew. Small in stature and timid, emotional, three strikes against me."

"Children are meant to be protected, not groomed to be killers."

"True. I became the apprentice to The Order's librarian. It is a great honor to earn an appointment to the position. Although it was a temporary one until chosen to be—" Lark ceased speaking as she stared off into space and raised her hand to swipe at the tickling of tears down her cheeks. "I made myself indispensable, took great pride in my work. A few months before I escaped, Reginald, one of the highest-ranking Hunters cornered me and told me I was to be his."

"Lark, that's not your life or purpose anymore, you have so much more to offer."

"What do I have if I don't have my mate? I can have a full life, work, Meadow, I don't think I can be satisfied if I lose her."

"I won't let that happen. Amora has you, someone that's hers and that above all else is a reason for her to fight to come home. Finding her siblings is something she has to do, even if the chance is small, she has to know. Amora thought they died and she was alone. I think in some ways that destroyed her more than the years of torture. Amora is resilient, refuses to show weakness, but just in the small amount of time, I have seen her with you, Amora's different. I can't say she's settled, she never will be, I think you gave her something she never thought to have."

"What's that? Yvette said something similar."

"Family, Lark, my grandparents instilled a strong sense of family. She feels she failed in protecting her brother and sisters. It was her task to keep them safe. Amora brought your sister home alive and happy, that soothed her some. Finding Nicolette and the others I think would rid her of the guilt."

"Then it's what she has to do, and I won't take that from her." Lark forced a bit of happiness to show she didn't feel and from the look in Ripper's eyes he knew she was only putting on a brave front.

"When Amora comes home, make sure you let her know you'll be here waiting for her when her mission is done. Someone once told me being the mate of a great warrior comes with far more peril and heartache than being the warrior going into battle."

"Seamus?"

"That old Alpha is pretty wise, and he's not wrong. Amora will know you're here with Meadow and safe, you won't have the same luxury." With those parting words, Ripper left her to her thoughts, troubled as they may be and she sighed heavily. She played the words over in her head, knowing Ripper was right didn't change the fact she wanted to beg her mate to stay.

So much bloodshed and pain, how much longer must the war go on before they found peace? How many times must they be moved like pawns on a chessboard sacrificed for Kali's amusement? So many questions, yet still unanswered. Amora would go back to the castle, she would fight and eventually get the information from the Council. Lark could only pray that her mate would come home with the answers that would give her the peace she required.

CHAPTER 20

Thirty minutes ago, she'd walked among the mausoleums and tombstones with the long dead and the energy of the deceased surrounding her. Now, it was a morgue and the Crypt Keeper herself. The once celebrated guide for the newly dead, she now locked herself away in a basement cutting them to pieces.

"Ennis, as ghoulish as always." Amora smirked and stepped out of the shadows. The stench of death and antiseptic wrinkled her nose. The nondescript elderly lady turned and squinted at her through the thick lenses of black rimmed glasses.

"Cut the shit, vamp, what the hell do you want?"

Ennis turned with a graceful flare that sent the white coat billowing around her small body. Like with a majority of creatures of the night, the nastiest always bore the most innocent facades. Amora slipped her hands into the front pockets of her jeans and approached the autopsy table.

"I love a woman who knows her way around a scalpel."

"You love a woman if she's breathing and wet."

"Ennis, you break my heart." Amora removed her hands from her pockets and placed them flat on her chest.

The woman waved the blade in Amora's direction. "There'd have to be one in there for it to break."

"You know if you weren't old enough to be my grandmother, I'd find the blade-wielding hot."

"You're a sick woman, Amora, been that long since you got a piece?"

"I get plenty." She wasn't sure if Ennis knew of Lark, but she wasn't going to show her hand if she didn't have to.

"Not that I don't live for these moments of intellectual banter, what do you need?"

"I need to find Epoch."

"Nasty bit of business there."

"Desperate times and all that bullshit. I went to the cemetery, he wasn't there, and there weren't any recently disturbed graves."

"Got himself locked away in a nuthouse."

"He can tear a body apart with his bare hands in a matter of seconds...no one can keep him locked up."

"Can if he's starving and weak."

"What happened?"

"Disturbance call by a nosy maintenance man. Police arrived as Epoch is starting in on his snack."

"I'm sure the cops loved that one."

"Yeah, they didn't appreciate the delicacy of fatty fingers. Long story short, no fingerprint match, he refuses to give his name, and the whole cannibal thing gets him a nice little padded cell with three-squares a day."

"Where?"

"Experimental treatment facility just outside the city limits. High security and heavily armed guards."

"Sounds like a walk in the park. Got a little snack I can take for our little friend?"

"Rich philanthropist came in. He donated his body to science. I'm sure he wouldn't mind giving up his pound of flesh for a good cause and all that."

"Knew there was a reason I worshiped you."

"Still not getting in my panties, Amora, that ship sailed about two hundred years ago."

"You tried to feed me to Epoch."

"You were trespassing."

"I was just doing a job, and he ignored the fact he owed me one."

"Wait here, I'll get Epoch his treat. I know his favorite parts." Ennis shuffled off into another room.

Maybe this wasn't exactly a good idea. Sometimes when the past comes back to bite you in the ass an old, even entirely demented ally was better than none. When she'd escaped from Kali's Order, she'd found him in a cell not far from hers. Their acquaintance lasted just passed the basilica walls, but she hadn't left him locked up to starve to death.

Amora pivoted when she sensed Ennis behind her. "Here." Amora took the bag and inspected it. "Are you freeing him?"

"That's up to him. He might like his new arrangements."

"A disgusting creature, he stopped eating fresh meat a long time ago, but the sin still stains the soul."

"You want him back?"

"Of course, the best guard I ever had. Works exceptionally cheap."

"If he decides to leave I'll drop him off."

"Try not to kill anyone, Amora, if I weren't immortal the overtime alone would kill me."

"Behave, and I'll retrieve your pet."

Amora tucked who knows what under her arm and ambled toward the door.

"Amora," Ennis called her name.

She paused and turned back. "Yeah?"

"Don't be such a stranger, us old pariahs need to stick together in dangerous times such as these."

"Something I need to know?"

"Rumors of a changing of the guard is imminent, and the free thinkers and rule-breakers aren't welcome."

"So same shit, different century."

"Exactly."

"Thanks."

She disappeared back into the shadows and out into the muggy night. Another mission without a plan in place. Amora needed to stop making a habit of that. It wasn't just her any longer, Ripper would avenge her and then move on as she'd taught him to do. But Lark and Meadow—those two were a different story. She couldn't leave her mate behind. Life hadn't hardened the innocence Lark exuded. Growing up in The Order had only begun to leave callouses of disillusionment. Being Amora's mate wouldn't be easy, but she'd protect Lark to the death.

She opened her car door and slid into the driver's seat. She stowed the package on the passenger seat and then started the engine. Amora pulled away from the curb. The trip to the facility didn't take long. She shut off the lights and slowed to a stop close to the gate. Two armed guards patrolled on either side. Reaching into the back seat, she picked up her bag, removed her blades, then shoved the package inside.

With a quick check of the time—just about shift change. It wouldn't completely conceal her, six-plus foot of redhead wasn't inconspicuous at all. She exited the car and slipped on the backpack. Amora jogged to the line of trees along the security fence. Jumping over it was easy, and the stroll across the grounds was too easy. She had to admit she was disappointed. The few guards she'd encountered she'd heard them coming, heavy steps and jingling keys. Although, the tech impressed her. High dollar, weird for what she'd assumed was a state-run facility.

Less speculating and more movement. Get in and get out, maybe with Epoch in tow. She didn't care for cells and locked doors, she'd spent too much time in them. Amora tilted her head back and studied the six floors, scaling the wall wouldn't take long. She quickly climbed the exterior and launched herself the last twelve feet to land in a crouch on the flat roof. Cigarette smoke tickled her nose, and she spotted a shadow on the far side.

A block of wood propped open the door. She crept toward it and slipped inside unnoticed. Her boots didn't make a sound as she descended the steps and slipped out onto the third floor. She needed a computer.

A deserted nurses' station with dim lights was positioned at the end of the corridor. She slipped inside, she hesitated and listened, no one—staff or patients—appeared to be housed there. Powering up the computer, she leaned down and stupidly she didn't need to enter a password. Something about the place was making her uneasy. They had one patient listed as John Doe. Just what she needed, he was in the basement.

Now or never, she took off at a run before the panic of small, dark spaces threatened to choke her. The quickest route was the elevator, but if security monitored those, they'd know someone had infiltrated the facility—steps were better. Amora skidded to a stop at the basement exit and checked through the small window. Dress shoes clacked against linoleum, wasn't a nurse, definitely not a guard. A doctor with a security card she'd probably need.

Again, it was too simple, missions with no snags never worked out in her favor. Three, two, one, Amora jerked open the door and gripped the old man's throat.

"Where is John Doe?" Amora demanded.

"Wh-Who?" The man reeked of fear and cheap cologne.

"Don't fuck with me, where is he?"

"Down the hall, B Ward, Room 6, but he's—"

"Yeah, dangerous, a biter, where's the key for his room?"

The doctor's hand shook as he patted the front pocket of his traditional dress shirt.

"I'll go ahead and take that, you didn't see me, right?"

"Rig—" She slammed his head against the wall and let him crumble to the floor.

It shocked Amora that the human race survived so long. Fragile creatures, she rumbled low in her chest and quickly strode to room six. She swiped the card, the lock beeped, and she used her bag to prop the door open.

"Well, hello, Ms. Jackyl, what a pleasure to see you again." A pleasant male voice came from the darkness and a slight male with a baby face stepped into the halo of a single overhead light.

Amora knew the beast beneath the unassumingness. The perfect camouflage, he barely looked more than eighteen. Without the striped scrubs with inmate across the chest, he could pass for younger. Another perfect weapon.

"Epoch, is there a reason you haven't busted yourself out of here yet?"

"It's rather enjoyable actually, these humans are so cute and—naïve. The menu leaves a lot to be desired though. That doctor believes he can diagnose me, can you imagine what would happen to his tiny brain if he knew?"

"The nerve of the human and about that menu." She kept her back to the wall and squatted to unzip her bag. "Ennis sent you a treat." She tossed it in his direction.

"Are you still holding a grudge?"

"Of course not, still on the fresh meat wagon?"

"We're more than instinct, Amora, we're not slaves to our cravings."

"So I should take your pound of flesh back?"

"Of course not, there's only so much clean living. So, why have you broken into a facility for the criminally insane?"

"The Order of Angelus."

"So you've discovered that you didn't kill them all."

"You knew?"

"Of course, humans are all about breeding. They fuck, shit out more replicas to mold into perfect little machines, like shampoo, rinse and repeat, procreation by number. Man's obsession with mortality, it's all rather sad really."

"Why did they originally take you?"

"For the reason they took all of us, weapons. We were predisposed to violence. You were from a warrior class of vampires, I revert into a mindless killing machine when starved. Anyone in my path becomes my meal. Except vampires, of course, your meat tastes stale. Distasteful, but beggars can't be choosers."

"Were there others?"

"Plenty, most didn't survive. High rates of suicide. Extermination if they failed to reach the level of violence sufficient to satisfy the Elders. They kept us for training purposes also. We were captured at the infancy of their creation. Their Hunters needed to know the enemy. Although they didn't anticipate the full capabilities of a Vampire Warrior, or maybe they did. You are possibly their greatest accomplishment and failure."

"Yeah, yeah, I'm the pinnacle of an insane killer."

"There has probably never been a truer statement made."

"You like your new digs, our Ennis is missing you."

"Such a lovely woman." He sighed.

"So, you ready to get out?" She hid a grimace as he hugged his package to his chest and rocked from side to side. So creepy and oddly cute.

"Yes, please. I grow bored with the arrangement."

"Then after you." She motioned for him to precede her with a bow and a sweep of her arm.

"You are untrusting, Amora." He tsked at her.

"You attempted to gnaw my throat out."

"One little bite, it barely left a scar. Such a baby."

"I have to be certifiable."

"More so than me, Amora, I assure you."

"Don't insult your rescuer."

"Is the truth an insult?"

Amora shook her head as he shuffled away. She knew she was going to regret this and just added it to the continuously expanding list.

* * *

AMORA CLOSED the door behind her as sunlight started to chase out the gloominess of the alley. The loft was quiet, and memories of what drove her away came back.

"I was wondering if you were coming home."

She turned to find Lark standing in the space between two screens. Her mate was beautiful. Lark wore one of Amora's t-shirts, and it barely reached the tops of sexy thick thighs. "I'm—" Amora paused. She closed the distance between them and leaned down to kiss Lark. Lark backed up and pinched her nose.

"What is that stench?" The nasally question almost made Amora smile—almost.

"Ghoul," Amora answered.

"Do I even want to know?"

"Probably not, I'm going to shower and then come to bed."

"Good idea, I'll be waiting for you." Lark kissed her quickly and then backed into their room.

"It's not that bad." It probably was, but she'd blocked it out.

"You smell like roadkill."

"Thanks, I spent the evening helping a ghoul escape, he nearly bit me again, and I reek like roadkill." Amora threw her hands up and marched to the bathroom. "There is no love left in this relationship."

"I'll love you more when you don't stink."

Amora slammed the door and leaned back against it. The more she learned, the less she realized she knew. She was tired of The Order and Kali, she wanted her decent homicidal life back. Death she understood, but the regular family stuff—completely clueless. She needed a shower, a drink and bed.

Amora had a mission and then a life to plan with Lark.

CHAPTER 21

The trepidation was thick as they waited. The presence of Hunters and guards had doubled. Ripper and Amora didn't speak, just hid in the shadows waiting for the change of shifts. Lark and Meadow were at the forefront of her thoughts, yet she needed to push them to the back. There was too much at stake for her to be distracted. Once again, she hadn't promised her mate she would come home. The sadness in Lark's eyes when they'd said goodbye begged her to stay.

If a chance remained that her siblings lived, she needed to know. Even if they confirmed they were dead, maybe not the night of the fire but later on, she had to have proof. The uncertainty would eat away at her otherwise. Ripper nodded in the darkness as a bell tolled the change of guard.

With nearly silent whispers of steps, they skirted the dim lights of spotlights and lanterns. They didn't enter the same way Amora had the first time. Instead, they circled to the rear and scaled the wall with lightning speed. Landing on top of the battlement, the first leg of their journey was smooth, and they remained undetected until they entered the castle through a large wooden door.

Creaking hinges were unusually loud as they opened it, and pulled it closed behind them. Speaking was unnecessary as their plan was already in place to follow. Amora took the lead, Ripper at her back as they traversed the corridors. The lack of internal security raised the hair on the back of her neck. The human presence was lower than it had been, and with a sick feeling, she realized they had moved the castle occupants elsewhere. She darted a look over her shoulder and could see the acknowledgment in Ripper's gaze.

Anger flashed through her veins as they continued until they reached the library. Inside, Amora stood in the middle closing her eyes as she focused. She attempted to sense someone that wasn't supposed to be there. The pungent scent of herbs and spices perfumed the room, she scented the air, and on light feet, she headed toward an interior wall. She placed her palms on the thick, rough-textured fabric and pulled it to the side. A door hidden behind, she motioned with her head for Ripper to open it. Amora held up her hand and counted off three with her fingers. On three, Ripper pulled the door open as the lock and hinges gave under his strength. The thick smoke she'd scented covered the stench of sulfur and ash.

A dark robed male turned to them with narrowed eyes. "Ah, Amora Jackyl, you have returned, what a pleasure." His smile, although tight, was pleasant looking. Yet the wizen old man would fool the casual observer. He didn't confuse her; she could see the base excitement in his dark gaze.

"Dominic?" Her voice gave nothing away, flat and cold, she would not give the old demon the satisfaction of an emotional response.

"Yes, and I can assume that this young man is Rache, grandson of Kali, the prophesied one." Ripper's jaw ticked in her peripheral as the demon sneered his pleasure.

"My siblings survived, I want to know where they are."

"Do you dare to make demands?"

"Yeah, I dare, because I might not be able to get the information out of you, but my son sure as hell can." Ripper remained silent at her side, his fist reflexively clenched as he tried to reign in his demon that fought to get out.

"No need to be so hasty to violence, *vampire*." He made the word an insult, and she stepped deeper into the room. "I adamantly opposed the killing of your family, yet Kali overruled my objections."

"What do you know of my parents' murders?"

"Please, come in, it has been so long since I have had a conversation. They keep me rather cooped up in this old cell." She and Ripper remained where they stood. "Suit yourself. Kali sensed your power, Amora, he knew if he bred you to Demonus you would give birth to the most amazing weapon. A civilization killer, a means to enslave the world and said weapon would be only under his control. You and Demonus very much threw his plan into chaos. He expected the child to be raised by him while you and Demonus would no longer be of this realm or any other."

"Are you saying that he planned to kill his son?"

Dominic lowered his falsely feeble frame into a chair in front of the fire.

"Very much so, Demonus was weak. He was not willing to do what they expected and would be done away with after the deed was done."

"What did all this have to do with killing one Pure-born family? There were and are several others in possession of more power than the Jackyl family. We were nowhere near being at the top of the Pure-born food chain."

"Ah, but you are wrong, Amora. Your family was head of the Council, your father fell in love with one not meant for him. Helena was an anomaly, a very powerful and secret bloodline. Decreed by the Council as an Untouchable, idiotically thought to be inferior when she was anything but. You, Amora, you bear the gift of your mother, a warrior born. The means to end a war raging since the beginning of time. A female vamp meant to lead nations. What are you instead? A vengeful and cruel creature."

"What the fuck are you going on about?"

"Kali knew, and he was going to possess the greatest scourge this realm would ever see. The mixed breed of Pure-born Vamp and Soul Collector. An unstoppable force, you and Demonus gave him exactly what he wanted. Alas, what he wanted was securely kept from him, and Rache's hatred is only another obstacle."

"Why would they kill my mother's family?" Ripper asked.

"Very simple, young demon, they refused to part with their precious daughter. Kali tried to purchase you for a very fair price. When Samuel and Helena refused, he carried out his only other option. Kill them all and take what he needed."

"Are my brother and sisters still alive?"

A chuckle echoed off the walls as he adjusted his robe and settled farther back in the chair. "What would knowing they still exist do for you?"

"Don't fucking play with me, old man. Do they still live?"

"I know what you seek, and whom. Nicolette still exists. Naomi didn't survive the inferno. Where she is, I don't possess that particular knowledge. Your recent war has substantially declined the number of our Hunters. Kali is looking to settle yet another score with you, Amora. What will you do when he comes for you? Because don't doubt he will."

"I don't care if he comes for me and I know he will, it's only a matter of time. When he does, I will fight to the death for what is mine."

"You are a brave if a somewhat foolish woman, Amora. Your emotions will be your downfall. The book on the edge of the table, it possesses all we know of your precious family and the last known whereabouts of your sister."

"Why are you talking so freely?" Amora motioned Ripper to pick up the book as she watched the ancient demon as he stared into the flames.

"It matters not why I do it. We will see each other again. There are many questions that you will need answered. Kali keeps me trapped here, imprisoned. I am no more than a keeper of records, of histories, Kali would rather never see the light of day. Freedom, Amora, that is why I speak with you. I want my freedom and one day you and your son will give me that gift."

"How—" Dominic lifted his hand to halt her question, and she arched a brow at him.

"There is no answer to your question. One day you will need me, and you will return here. Now, go, the carnage you so crave isn't going to happen this night. It will though, Amora, you and your family have many battles ahead before the final act of war. Prepare and prepare well, Medina-Jackyl, because Hell is coming."

"Amora, let's go." Ripper grabbed her arm as the pounding of feet and voices raised in anger became louder.

"Beware who you trust, Amora, sometimes the sweetest face hides the bloodiest secrets." It was the last thing she'd heard before the strange tingling sensation moved outward from her stomach and along her limbs. Her stomach clenched and her head went light as they materialized back at her home.

"Goddammit, Ripper, I hate when you do that!" She jerked her arm from his steely-gripped fingers.

"If I didn't, we'd be fighting for our lives."

"So what, now, your bastard of a grandfather knows we were there."

"He already knew, there are no high-tech alarms in that place, someone warned them we were there, and I'm damn sure it was Kali."

"Amora!" She barely had time to brace herself before she was mowed over by her beautiful mate. "You're back! What happened? Did you even go in? Are you hurt? Do you need to feed?"

"Easy, baby, I'm all right, we've got more questions than answers now. Something's not right and that Dominic didn't make sense at all. Ripper, did you get the book?"

"Yeah, you told me to get it, and you saw me—" Ripper bent in half as she popped him in the stomach with the back of her hand. "Here, I'm going to my room, well, the one I share now, my new sister better not be a snorer." Her son huffed as he quietly stomped his feet to the second screen concealed bedroom where Meadow slept.

"What happened?"

"Will you look through this for clues to where to find Nico?" Amora held Lark close, not wanting to let her go.

"Of course, I'll study it while you're asleep tomorrow, now come to bed." She allowed Lark to lead her to their bedroom, but her mind was back in the castle still surrounded by the sickening stench of hell cloaked in the sweet musk. What if all that Dominic claimed was true? So many questions needed answering. She stripped and slipped into bed next to her mate, and wrapped the woman in her arms.

"I love you, Amora." The words were whispered warmly against the side of her neck, and her arms tightened as the now familiar sense of peace settled over her. She had yet to say the words to Lark, there was still too much ambiguity to what the future held. Her mate didn't demand the phrase, but she did deserve them, to hear them said aloud.

"I love you too, Lark—" An arm tightened around her, and soft lips pressed to hers. "I should have—" Another kiss shut her up.

"No, you said them when you were ready, and I wouldn't ask anything else. Now sleep, there's a lot to be done."

Lark rested her head on her chest, and a sigh caressed her skin. If her siblings survived, she needed to find them. So many years lost and too many mistakes made, Amora wasn't wasting another minute. Family was everything, and you never left one fallen in battle. Staring up at the ceiling, she listened to her mate's heartbeat become slow and even in sleep. Amora savored the warmth and serenity. For the first time, she felt that everything would work out, no matter what the hell they would battle through in the future. Everything would finally be set right.

CHAPTER 22

$\mathcal{M}$ iddle of the night calls weren't a good sign, yet nothing seemed natural anymore. Lark observed Amora, taking in her tensed shoulders and the low, dangerous rumble of her voice. A part of her wished for more time with just Amora and her, along with Meadow but she understood the need to protect. She knew her life with her vampire would be mostly high alerts and battles ending in blood and death.

The call ended, Amora's lean body pivoted, and even she was frightened by what she saw in the enraged black eyes.

"We have to go," Amora snarled.

"Where? What's wrong?"

Her mate seemed to notice the fear in her voice and the change was shocking. The once hardened and angry visage changed and the tall vamp approached to wrap Lark in her arms. "You remember the night we met?"

"You mean the one where you tried to make me into a snack."

"That's the one."

"What about it?"

"I brought Ada to Seamus for protection. His pack isn't like others, he'll accept anyone who's in need of help, and it's the reason I found her a home there."

"Is she no longer welcome? Do we need to bring her home with us?" It didn't bother her, she didn't hesitate to offer Ada a haven. Instinctively, she knew it was exactly what Amora would do.

"No, I fucked up. I came across her while I was on a job. Turned vampires are strictly regulated. If someone turns someone without—" Amora paused.

Powerful, slender hands stroked her back in a gentle up and down motions.

"I didn't know there were rules."

"I normally say fuck the rules, I do my own thing, and no one fucks with me. Unfortunately, there's a Council who takes this seriously, and they contacted me to use as a subcontractor of sorts—have done so in the past. A vampire named Boone was turned a few hundred years ago and has been leaving a bloody trail ever since. He's a sadistic, mass murderer, and I let him get away."

"How?"

"I saw what he did to Ada, you saw her?" Lark nodded in answer. "It became more than a job, a bounty to make. She needed to be avenged. I've killed plenty, some I regret and others I enjoyed. I tortured Boone, marked him with the exact wounds he left on Ada, and then I staked him in the yard with special rope. A witch I know helped me out with it. It seems someone or something freed him. Ada swears he's following her."

"She's traumatized, and her mind may be playing tricks on her."

"Possibly, but I need to know for sure. Pack for a few days, we have to make a stop first to talk to an old acquaintance. Whatever she says or does, don't let her get to you."

"Am I about to meet one of your—" Lark didn't even have to finish the question. The tiny twitch under Amora's left eye was answer enough. "Great, let me get us packed, and Meadow dressed." She pulled away and instantly regretted it when the shadows overtook Amora's features—the physical retreat. Her lover pulling away felt in the tightening of her stomach and chest. Lark thought about apologizing, to stroke gently over Amora's face, but she didn't have time before Amora was gone.

Lark pushed a heavy sigh passed her lips and hung her head. She'd fallen hard for the monster The Order created. She knew she wasn't strong or mercenary, passive and submissive were her burdens to bear, and she wondered, in the end, would it be enough.

* * *

A SWEET, smoky scent of incense teased her nose, Lark couldn't place the smell, yet it seemed familiar. She shook off the odd feeling and stepped through the doorway into the cluttered occult shop. Instead of bringing Meadow, Amora decided the little girl would be safer with Seamus and Yvette, so they arrived to see Amora's old friend a day later than planned. She tried to appear relaxed, but inside it was chaos.

Soft tapping drew her attention to the back of the shop where an ancient looking woman with flowing white hair and a tunic stepped from the shadows. The sound of the cane grew louder, and her stare met faded, cloudy blue eyes.

"Jackyl." It was said in an icy, cracked tone.

"Selena."

Amora's voice as equally cold, but held a lethal edge. The former lovers didn't appear friendly.

"Who's this beautiful morsel?" The old voice changed suddenly to a smooth, sexy rasp and Lark felt a strange pull to approach—to touch.

Amora's suddenly wrapped her arm around her waist and tugged her close to Amora's side. "You even think about fucking touching her, and I'll kill you. I'm not here for your games."

"You used to like my games and the marks I'd leave."

"Save the bullshit, Selena."

Lark observed the standoff, and for some reason she found the tall, powerful Amora staring down the stooped, old Selena funny.

"You're amused, why?"

"You're thinking about tearing grandma apart."

"And you find that funny," Amora drolly stated, but the glint of amusement in Amora's blue eyes made her smile wider.

"Yep."

"Quit eye-fucking each other. What do you want?"

"Testy, I need you to read for me." She'd explained to Lark that she'd made the request in the past and Selena denied her each time, but this one was different.

"No, I can't discern your future, Amora, people shouldn't know certain things about themselves."

"Not for me, I need to know where to find someone, and you can connect to him through me."

"And why should I help? Perhaps another ride for old time's sake?"

Lark stiffened and then watched the old woman shift and change into a beautiful, lithe blonde with twinkling ice blue eyes. An over-whelming sense of sorrow and rage infused her as her inadequacies gut-punched her. All the air left her lungs suddenly. Would Amora take Selena up on the payment for information? She wanted to hope no, but the other woman was hauntingly beautiful. Lark shook her head wondering where the sudden doubt and anger came in and felt Amora stiffen at her side.

"Quit, Selena, knock down the charm, apologize," Amora ordered.

"Wow, when did an innocent face put the Great and Murderous Amora on a choke chain?"

"I just need the information, don't cause me to make you wish for death before I get what I want."

"Fine, holding this form tires me out. That fucker knew what he was doing when he only made me beautiful to men. I would kill for soft curves and the taste of feminine arousal on my tongue."

"What?" Lark was asking the question before she knew it.

"A long time ago, I told a high-level demon no, he tried to take what I wasn't willing to give, and I imprisoned him. Being a powerful witch has its perks."

"She wouldn't let him out until he learned his lesson, but as a few years passed and he still proclaimed he'd take her willing or not, she figured the battle was lost. Selena let him out, he changed her."

"I, unfortunately, require men to continue my existence. Feeding off them during sex, since I'm not interested in males of any species it's a form of torture. I am only beautiful to men and women see me as you do now."

"But you just changed."

"Yes, but—" Selena's sigh was weary and filled with pain. "It's taken a long time to shift even for a few minutes, it drains me too quickly and requires me to find a male to replenish sooner than I want."

"Is there anything that can be done?" She looked between the women, and the grim expressions were answer enough.

"She's a sweet one, my old friend, is she crazy? Because that's the only way you could ever touch something so pure."

"Listen, witch, she doesn't have to change to touch me. Now cut your shit and tell her what we need to know." The rage slowly ebbed away, cleared her confused mind, and she found herself between Amora and Selena. The witch looked shocked, and Amora laughed loudly behind her. Selena wasn't looking at her though, but at Amora. Lark glanced over her shoulder and smiled at the amusement that changed Amora's features from dangerous to beautiful.

"Calm down, love." Amora lowered her voice, strong arms twined around her waist, and Amora's mouth brushed her ear. "Although you defending me was pretty sexy. I'll reward you later."

Lark squeaked and tightened her thighs. "Okay."

"You took a mate." Selena's awe-filled voice broke through Lark's haze of lust.

"Why is that so surprising?" Lark asked.

"The Monster doesn't deserve a mate, sins and blood can't be washed away. She doesn't—" A hysterical light flashed in Selena's eyes. Small, gnarled fists clenched at Selena's sides. The rage seemed misplaced, and Lark didn't understand why.

"Chaps your ass, doesn't it, witch?" Amora asked.

"Come in the back, but leave your pet out here." Selena smoothly pivoted belying her stooped and aged body.

Lark darted a glance over her shoulder to Amora. She didn't want her vamp to leave her behind.

"I know what you're thinking, but it'll be okay. This shouldn't take long, and then we can get back to Meadow."

She didn't have any choice but to agree and accept the quick kiss. Amora strode toward the back and Lark wrapped her arms around her stomach. Left to her own thoughts, once again doubts began to creep in. Was she ready to face the life ahead of her? There was so much at stake, Amora would protect their family with her life, and Lark's greatest fear was to find herself living the rest of her days without her lover.

With an effort, she blocked out the subtle drone of Amora and Selena's voices and lost herself in her head. This wasn't what she'd thought fate had in store for her when she'd escaped The Order. She'd searched out the Monster the cult created for the mere fact of releasing Meadow from years of servitude to false Gods. Lark didn't know if it was Selena screwing with her head again or something else —an ominous omen of the hell to come.

Changing or denying the love she felt for Amora was impossible, but could she handle the fear of losing her without breaking? Would she wake up one day to find her beautiful vampire no longer there beside her and the only memories she possessed weren't enough to sustain her until she drew her final breath? Lark turned away to hide the tears burning her eyes and wallow in a momentary despair until she had to be brave for her mate.

CHAPTER 23

*M*idnight drew near, and Seamus' camp still teemed with activity, music played softly. Humans and creatures danced within the flickering light of the fire. Amora took it all in on some level, yet her thoughts were on the reading she'd received from Selena. The details were vague, riddles to put Dominic to shame, but the only clear information was Boone still existed. Amora deceptively relaxed on a soft pallet and reclined into a mass of brightly colored pillows.

The ropes should've held and delivered him to his fate. No one should've succeeded in releasing Boone. In her gut, she knew Kali had a hand in releasing the turned vamp, yet to what end, she hadn't a clue. Other than Boone's penchant for cruelty and death, he served no purpose and Kali had plenty of men under his rule who exceeded the vamp's skills.

"What's going on in your head?" Lark's concerned voice broke through the chaos of Amora's thoughts.

"It doesn't make sense Boone coming after Ada, he's already done his damage." She reached out for Lark's hand, her mate took it, and she tugged Lark down into the curve of her side.

"Maybe he's mad? You said he was a sadist. What's to say Boone just doesn't want to revisit his crime and revel in the beauty he so-called destroyed." Lark cuddled in, and Amora held her tighter.

"It's more than that. Yes, he's fucking insane, but coming after Ada again while she's under my protection and that of Seamus? No one fucks with his pack, and everyone knows it. He has no qualms about going to war for those he considers pack."

"You two have a lot in common. Neither do you, but what if that's the plan? War, to draw you and Seamus in—to distract you."

"If someone wants war there are easier ways. Why use an innocent girl?"

"How well do you know this Council?" Lark asked.

"As well as anyone else, when preternatural creatures, angels, zombies, whatever they establish the rules to follow. Their reign began back in the Dark Ages, during the Crusades and the plague outbreak bodies started turning up, some appeared drained. The people needed someone to blame, the clergy used the excuse of witches, but the Council knew different. Although witches were like everyone else, good and bad, some of the preternatural became opportunistic. Crimes easily disguised under the cloak of illness or the Devil's Brides. The powers that be decided to get strict."

"How?"

"Rumors are...Dominic in his way confirmed it...they trained a group of elite warriors who could blend easily among Knights. Again, it's all fucking speculation. If we're anything, we're secretive and adept at hiding."

"So you don't believe they formed their own police force?"

"It's possible, human hunters have been around since before the invention of God or other deities."

"But could humans take down beings so much stronger than themselves?"

"In numbers, yes. But one on one? Their training would have to be exemplary, and I don't see humans surviving those battles. Bodies would've amassed in staggering numbers."

"Why don't they think humans and the preternatural could coexist?"

"Mass hysteria, the panic would spread, and in some ways, I think it would be the same as if aliens were found to exist. Humans believe they are the only intelligent species out there. What do you think would happen if humans discovered there were species out there stronger and faster—similar or identical in appearance?"

"Fear," Lark answered.

"Exactly, we could rule quite quickly, humans outnumber us, but we have superior strength. Yes, we have our weaknesses, but the movies don't get it right. Vampires can survive in the sun in small doses, unless we're forced to remain in the rays, we sustain minuscule damage. Cloudy days we have a bit more leeway."

"But The Order and the day at the motel—"

"Direct sunlight is harmful."

"What about silver for weres?"

"Same premise, unless it hits a vital organ they survive. It does slow healing, but other than that it's as dangerous as a human being shot or stabbed. The Full Moon is bullshit, weres can change at any time, but even though the pull of the Lunar Cycle is high, they still control when they become their animal.

"Yes, we can live for unknown life spans. Vampires can live a thousand years or more. Especially when they hibernate."

"Hibernate, like bears?"

"Sort of, some vampires have gone mad by living too long, seeing too much. We find humans to love, only to watch them slowly die, and turning a mate is against Council Law."

"So, you'll have to watch me—" Amora saved her from having to finish.

"No, one day I'll claim you completely, I refuse to lose you. But if what Dominic said is true, there may be a loophole."

"What is it?"

"He said the Medina-Jackyl's were head of the Council at one time, which means if I challenge it, we can once again rule."

"You don't want to govern. You'd never be left in peace."

"Lark, you're wrong, you're my peace, and I'd fight whatever battle I need to in order to keep you by my side."

"Where's the heartless monster The Order created?"

"I can't deny the monster I am. The idealistic child my parents raised died the moment I watched my home burn with my family inside. Vengeance runs through my veins, it colors all decisions, except for the one I made to love and claim you. I can't throw aside the vow I made the day I escaped, no matter how long it takes, I'll kill them all or die trying.

"My promise of forever isn't set in stone, Lark, I'll fight until I sever the head of the snake. I can't kill a demon, no one can. Kali can be banished, but if the prophecy is accurate, my son can and will kill Kali. Unfortunately, when that comes to pass my son has no choice, but to become what he despises most, a parasite."

"He told me that the first time I met him, he just needs more time."

"And in taking that time, we're cursed with endless battles and no war to win in sight. How many more of our Clan has to suffer or die before my son decides enough is enough?"

"Ripper has to make his way, Amora, you can't force him into a role he isn't ready for."

"Of that I'm aware. And as much as it pisses me off, his fate is his own."

"Just a bit longer, let him have it. We'll find Nicolette and the rest. I'm still studying, but I'm sure I can find something to lead us to her."

"I know, yet my patience grows thinner each day. If my past mirrors hers in any way, was she able to survive or did she fall to an enemy, or maybe her own hand? Too many times in my past I thought of throwing open the curtains and letting the sun in. I failed them, Lark, I was trained to protect my siblings, even if they didn't die, they did suffer because I couldn't—"

"You were a child. Yes, you were trained to take them to safety, yet you were still a child outnumbered. How many more years need to pass before you forgive yourself?"

"Until I know they still exist, there's no forgiveness for me." Amora knew Lark wanted to argue with her, but Amora's tone brooked no argument. Child or not, she'd failed in her task, and nothing she ever did would atone for that. Her family suffered and died for her weakness, there weren't excuses to wash that away—not even the love of the woman curled beneath her arm. Lark was hers, yet in some part of Amora's shattered soul, she still couldn't allow herself to believe she deserved the love she'd found. As Selena implied, the monster lived with too many sins to possess someone so innocent and loving.

CHAPTER 24

"I don't give a fuck, Ada, you're going to talk, and you're going to do it now," Amora roared in rage.

Lark really shouldn't find it so amusing or allow her mate to use profanity around Meadow, but tiny Ada glaring up at the lethal vamp anyone else would cower in front of was hilarious. She held Meadow on her lap, and the little girl watched Ada and Amora, her curls shifting as Meadow bounced back and forth between them.

"This is not fucking funny, Lark." Amora shot her a glance and Lark covered another laugh with a cough.

"Of course it's not." She hoped she was pulling off the somber expression, yet she knew her twinkling gaze was giving her away.

"Fight with your girlfriend some other time, I'm done, Amora. You took me from my home—"

"The whorehouse wasn't your home."

"Whatever, it's done, he's dead, and I'm crazy."

"Shut the fuck up, quit being so damn stubborn."

Ada's perfectly arched brow rose until it disappeared into the fringe of her bangs. "Are you high?"

Lark hid her face in Meadow's hair.

"Momma 'Mora, what's high mean?"

"See what you started? I didn't sign up to adopt two fucking kids. I already have one pain in the ass demon to deal with, and now I got you and Meadow. This family shit is for the birds."

"Have we forgotten your mate is barely legal?"

"She's twenty, dammit!"

"And you're how old? Let's do the math shall we?"

"When did you become such a smartass," Amora demanded.

"She'll fit right in, should I start planning her room?"

"Your complete adoration was a lie—a lie!"

"You know I love you." Lark smiled as she spoke.

She loved the way her mate's whole body seemed to ease. Lark didn't believe she'd ever get over the awe of being able to give Amora a small measure of peace. No matter the life they'd live, and all the chaos they'd face, she'd never regret her decision to search for the vicious vamp.

"Might as well, someone has to keep her in line."

"I'm not a child, I can take care of myself."

"Too damn bad, you're coming home with us. But first, we have to deal with whether Boone survived or not. What the hell did you see?" Amora asked.

Ada was about to refuse; Lark could see it in the stubborn line of the woman's jaw. After what Ada went through, the show of spirit was a good sign. Maybe Boone hadn't broken her completely, left a small part of the old Ada intact.

"Fine, Seamus made me go into town. Like I need to be looked at like a freak any more than I already am," Ada whispered.

Amora's arm went outward curling her slender fingers around the back of Ada's neck, and Lark held her breath.

"You're not a freak! What did I tell you? Repeat it for me."

"We're survivors."

"Exactly, scars don't make the measure of a person. They're physical reminders of what we've overcome."

Lark felt tears fill her eyes and a lump form in her throat. Family wasn't something she possessed before escaping The Order. Her parents saw children as a commodity—a simple duty to reproduce to grow their armies or breeding stock. She'd wanted more for Meadow, finding that with a Beast of The Order's making shocked her.

"Is Momma 'Mora and Auntie Ada, okay?"

"Yes, baby, they're fine. Just need to talk." She cuddled her sister closer. The staring contest wasn't getting them anywhere closer to finding if Boone was alive or a figment of Ada's imagination. "What did you see when you went to town?" Lark asked. Amora didn't release Ada, even when Ada briefly glanced at Lark and then dropped her chin to her chest.

"It wasn't quite dark yet, I felt like I was being watched. You know that feeling where the hair stands up on the back of your neck. Fuck, I hate being afraid. I checked all the shadows and swore I saw something moving. It was only a few minutes, but it was him—I know it was."

"How did he look? Did he appear injured in any way?"

"Half his face looked as if melted, but he smiled at me with that same smile. Cold and lustful, a promise that he was going to finish what he started. I can't—" A sob loudly sounded in the quiet of the large tent. "I can't do that, Amora, I can't survive it again. Watching pieces of yourself carved away, the sting of the blade almost painless before…the ripping as he pushes—"

Lark was about to cover Meadow's ears when Amora jerked Ada to her, holding her tightly while the young woman trembled in her mate's embrace. A soothing rumble and words of comfort slowly calmed Ada.

"Do you have any family, Ada?"

Ada shook her head before speaking. "No, I got them, but—" The young woman paused.

Lark couldn't take the aura of misery around Ada and stood, holding Meadow tight in her arms and approached the other two women. She tucked her baby sister between Amora and Ada, her mate instantly holding Meadow with one arm, and then Lark embraced all three. Both of them stiffened, and she couldn't help but smile. She had her work cut out for her.

"Yes, you have them, and we're right here. Come on, no more tears,

Amora is going to do her thing and take care of Boone. While she's doing that, we can make a list of stuff you'll need for when we go home."

When she finished, Amora's arm tightened around her waist and tugged her even closer.

"Lark." Amora only had to say her name to know it was a warning —a half-hearted one.

She stepped away, reaching for Meadow who had gone silent. "Play with your toys while I talk with Aunt Ada, okay?"

Meadow nodded, and Lark set her in one of the piles of pillows. When she turned her attention back to Amora, her mate had stepped back, and the weight of the vamp's gaze confused her.

"Don't promise me you'll come back," she spoke with more conviction than she felt.

"I wouldn't do that. I'll only make promises I can keep."

"Good enough, do I get one more night?"

"I have to make contact with Ripper and a few others. I'll be back in a few hours."

"Everyone will be safely tucked in."

Amora moved so fast it took Lark's breath away, and she savored the strength of her mate's embrace. "I have plans for you."

"I look forward to it," she said.

Lark would always have one more night and day of being in her mate's arms. She would always secretly crave the promise that Amora would always come back, but one day she may not. Surrendering wasn't in her vamp's makeup, she hadn't survived all these centuries by cowering and rejecting a fight. She turned her head, her cheek caressing over Amora's and then their mouths were a mere breath apart.

She lifted her right hand to stroke her fingertips along the smoothness of Amora's cheek and watched in fascination as her mate's lids fell to conceal her gaze. She didn't miss the longing in that one fleeting glimpse. The need and love Amora had for her left her in awe. That a dangerous and cold creature could feel that way about her. And she would do whatever she had to, to make sure it remained there. Lark knew her place in the world with Amora, it was by her side, taking care of their family when she went off to fight battles for others or their family.

With everything she believed...she was Lark, and she knew without a doubt that this was why she was created. There along with Amora and their extended Clan was where she belonged, and with that epiphany, every misgiving she ever carried about her inferiority evaporated.

She pushed upward on her toes, her lips conforming to the softness of her mate's and she tenderly kissed Amora. "I'll always be here waiting for when you come home, that's a promise I can keep."

Amora kissed her once more, then nodded and reluctantly released her. Lark wanted Amora to hold on just a little longer, but she let her vamp go with only a smile.

Lark was left alone with Ada and Meadow, the flaps of the tent barely moving with Amora's exit.

"What's it like to be loved like that?" Ada's softly whispered question held so much pain that it broke Lark's heart.

"It's amazing, and one day you'll find out." Ada shook her head. "Enough of that, we have to figure out what you need and to make lists. Would you like to set up your room?"

Lark asked the question and hoped to lighten to mood. The woman in front of her was only a few years older than herself, but she looked like a child with her head bowed. She couldn't fight the battles with fists and weapons like her mate, yet she could soothe and bring the young woman some happiness. Hopefully, Amora could make her feel safe and at peace when she took care of the bastard who attempted to break the newest member of the Jackyl Clan.

CHAPTER 25

*F*rustration seemed like second nature to Amora, yet she rarely let herself cave under it. After the supposed deaths of her family, she didn't allow herself to fail and once more she'd succeeded in doing just that—failing. She'd make sure the bastard was dead this time. She pushed through the soft covering of the tent entrance and stepped inside. A cheerful fire in the tall ceramic fire-place cast flickering lights among the shadows.

Amora slowly removed her clothes and neared the pallet toward the back of the enclosure. She found Lark curled under the covers— she looked so young and innocent. She'd thrown the sheltered woman into dangerous chaos, but she couldn't bring herself to send her away —to do what was probably right. Her selfishness knew no limits when it came to her mate. She crouched down, tugged at the corner of the blankets and threw them to the bottom of the makeshift bed.

A smirk tugged at the left corner of her mouth, and she lowered herself to lay beside Lark. Silky, lightly tanned skin exposed turning almost golden in the light of the fire. She loved the young woman and Amora hadn't thought it would happen, couldn't allow herself what she believed a weakness. Amora scooted closer to Lark, the warmth of her lover's body caused her to shiver in pleasure. She lifted her upper body, resting her weight on her forearm above Lark's head, and with agonizingly slow motions, reached out to caress her hand from Lark's shoulder to her sweetly plump thighs.

Her mate moved restlessly under her touch. Amora tweaked the small triangle of dark pubic hair and licked her lips as Lark arched her hips. Lark unconsciously turned, sliding her thigh over Amora's hip and she palmed the thick curve of Lark's ass cheek. She loved the softness—the curves—she never dreamed of so much kindness and innocence belonging to her alone. She slid her leg upward until her thigh firmly pressed to Lark's wetness. A tiny whimpering sigh drew her attention to the fullness of slightly parted lips. Her gums prickled as her long, sharp fangs elongated further.

She lowered her head to place nips to the curves of each lip, the corners and then to Lark's chin. Her mate arched her neck, exposing the elegant line and Amora's drew the tips of her incisors from soft jaw to the trembling pulse.

Lark moaned, and Amora sensed her slowly awakening.

"Amora," Lark moaned her name. "I love when you touch me, love me." The words broke and ceased as Amora sunk just the tips of her teeth into Lark's flesh. A mere sip was all she needed—for now.

"The feeling is mutual, I said I had plans for you, and this—" Amora huskily whispered. She eased her hand between Lark's thighs from behind. Amora lowered her leg for better access to skim the sweet part of Lark's lips, delving deeper until she pushed at the hot, wet entrance and breached her gently with two fingers. Wet silk contracted around the digits, and Amora felt an answering wetness pool between her legs.

Lark's hands stroked over her, touching every inch she could reach, and Amora noticed she paid closer attention to the scars, gentling her touch. That always alert, ready for danger feeling faded, disappearing and the peace only Lark could give her infused her battle fired synapses. She couldn't think of her enemies, the peril or the next battle ahead, her only focus was on the beautiful woman in her arms.

* * *

THE STENCH of rank body odor, fear and sex swirled into a disgusting, nauseating mix. A century ago what had seemed like a mass exodus of lost souls started appearing in the middle of a Mexico desert. A broken-down commune popped up. What the public didn't know was the collective protected one of four portals that brought the Lost Ones topside. Most called it Hell, but it was a shitty little realm of the worst of the worst. Not to say innocent creatures or humans didn't find themselves there. It was a prison of sorts, and as with any prison sometimes the inmates got out.

Humans weren't alone, some knew, but the majority slept better when they believed they were at the top of the food chain.

"This is the stupidest fucking idea you have ever had, Ma," Ripper hissed behind her.

Amora may even agree with her son, but she'd never admit it.

No one would let Ripper down there. But her, on the other hand, had free access, and for great reasons, she hadn't taken advantage.

"What? It'll be fun, like a school field trip, all educational and shit."

"Jackyl, look what the Devil dragged in." A lilting brogue pulled her attention away from her pissed off son. She hadn't seen the demon in years, but if she needed information or a guide, he was the one to see. There were few she trusted, and Kellan was on the shortlist.

Kellan was a reptile of some kind and one day, he was injured in battle and attempted to shift. Somehow, he'd become stuck in the in-between. Grayish-green bumpy skin mixed with the dark mahogany of his human side, one eye matched his rich brown hair and the other a vibrant yellow. He didn't spend much time topside, but occasionally the temptation drew him out.

"Kellan," she acknowledged him. His arm shot out, Ripper stepped forward, but before he could intervene Amora reached out. Her hand wrapped around Kellan's forearm as he did the same to hers.

"When I got the message from our mutual friend, I was rather surprised."

They squeezed once more and released each other, then Amora stepped back to stand beside Ripper. "Meet Rache." She pointed her thumb at Ripper. Kellan reached out to shake, and his arm was held suspended.

"Don't call me that," Ripper grumbled. "Kellan, call me Ripper."

She noticed Ripper ignored the extended hand. "Be nice," she warned.

Kellan dropped his arm back to his side.

"I'd rather be nice somewhere else."

"Not going to happen." She turned her gaze away from Ripper. "Did you make the arrangements for me?"

"He's waiting, but you know I tried to arrange it any other way. You're not the most popular down there, I'm just glad you scare them shitless."

"They should be frightened. Ferghus still holding a grudge?"

"You removed his arm with a sword and to make matters worse, you taunted him by beating him with the severed limb. That troll wants your head in the worst way."

Ripper groaned, and she turned her head to catch him rolling his eyes.

"What? I didn't know him and Greta had a thing, or we were in their house. She didn't mention it at any point before, during or after the fight. I apologized!"

"An apology works better if you're not laughing while you're doing it."

"I was young, a mere century, that's like vampire puberty."

"Same old Jackyl. I heard a rumor."

"Oh, and what's that?" Amora asked.

"You went and got yourself mated."

Amora tensed but hid it quickly. The preternatural gossip chain proved a dangerous and annoying occurrence. She should've known word of Lark would have already made it there. "Problem with that?"

"Not at all, means my ugly mug might have a chance."

"Same ol' asshole."

"We all have our talents. You ready for this?" Kellan asked.

"You're acting a little nervous," Amora teased.

"I'm leading the Infamous Amora Jackyl back below, I'm antici-pating a fight or a hundred."

"It'll be fine. You're losing your edge, my old friend. Besides this is the first time I'm thankful for my reputation."

"That may not save you this time, Jackyl, with your enemies around every corner you're on borrowed time."

"True, but I've been living on that borrowed time for centuries. I was born with an expiration date, I don't know when, but I know it's there. Every day is a good day to die, I just hope it's not today." The adage was bravado, Amora didn't have anyone to live for before. She and Ripper had a silent understanding—they both knew how easily their enemies could get to them. She now had Lark and Meadow, two innocents who needed her there. Amora Jackyl was known for her recklessness, cultivated a don't give a damn attitude, but no longer could she exist with her former abandon.

"Are we going to stand around and reminisce all fucking night or get this over with," Ripper muttered.

"Can't wait for the possible death wish mission," Amora stated with amusement.

"You're not the only one who has too much to lose, Ma."

Amora nodded in reply, her son had as much to lose as she does. Contrary to the fact he refused to claim his mate, Ripper couldn't bear to imagine never seeing the woman again. They'd spoken many nights of the fear he carried of his future—when prophecy couldn't be denied.

"Let's go." Amora squared her shoulders and gestured Kellan to go ahead. Friend or not, she wouldn't allow anyone at her back except her family. Some things would never change.

The crowd they walked into seemed to disperse, parting like a great sea and she felt hundreds of eyes following their every move.

"Did the stench of fear and loathing increase to sickening levels just now?"

Amora held in her chortles, she relished those smells. Fear and loathing combining into a sweet cloying mixture. Preternatural and humans alike could hide a lot, but not their scents. There was only one scent though that she loved above all others was Lark's—when the woman wanted her beyond madness or thought.

"Yep. The Medina-Jackyl Monster who hunts monsters and the next Soul Collector, get used to it, son, they'll fear us as much as they'd slit our throats at the first opportunity. Keep sharp and watch your six."

"Got it, you armed?"

"Rache, always." She grinned at the cute puppy-like rumble behind her. Ripper hated his name.

"This might be one of the few times I appreciate how deadly you are."

"Aw, son, I can feel the love."

"Shut up and keep focused. We find out Boone's whereabouts, and then we go back to our usual fucked-up existence."

"Agreed."

The atmosphere thickened the closer they drew near the portal. She steeled herself for the nauseating shifting of her molecules, and they pushed through the barrier. To anyone else, it would look as if they'd disappeared into an alley between two dilapidated buildings. The heat was the first thing she noticed, and then the familiar landscape of varying shades of crimson. Yeah, it looked like Hell, but that place was something of myth—a zealot's hallucination.

She leaned her head back to look up at the colossal towering walls of the city, Mael. It was like any other place, rotting from the ground up and teeming with the worst of the combined realms. Dangerous and only fit for criminals and the most damaged. Amora spent quite a few years walking the streets inside. There was a realm its exact opposite, but the inhabitants weren't inclined to leave those pristine, gilded walls.

Who'd want to leave paradise to live in the bowels of Mael? Okay, she'd do it, but she loved a little vice in her life. It wasn't like those chosen ones would hop down from their pedestal for a one-off. She could imagine the automaton missionary that went on there. She'd visited once, it was like clone central, ethereal white hair and startling blue eyes. Even the Chosen Ones had secrets, and she'd taken care of a few for them.

With Kellan in the lead, they approached the wrought iron gate. She felt a base sneer tug at the corners of her mouth at an all too familiar snarl. The force of a body hitting the metal rattled the hinges, and she stepped closer.

"Ferghus, how the hell ya doing?" Amora asked.

"You're crazier than I thought ya were to bring your ass back here." Vibrant yellow eyes with matching teeth, a great sloping forehead, and wide jaw pressed closer to the gate. The thick scars on his face didn't improve the picture.

"How's Greta?" Amora asked. Greta was a loose-limbed lovely Fae with a fetish for scars and rough sex. It was the only explanation for the troll boyfriend. Although Greta had a sadistic streak a mile wide, she wouldn't put it passed the female to play the act. Bring home an unsuspecting fuck for the night, just to anger the boyfriend. Amora was positive Greta hadn't expected Amora to do the damage she'd done.

"My woman is okay, you ain't welcome here, Jackyl."

"I gotta meeting with Demonus, ya can take it up with him." Shit, Amora was trying to keep that one under wraps until they made it to Demonus' place.

"What the fuck, Ma," Ripper bellowed behind her, yet she ignored him.

Okay, she'd deal with her son's anger later. Amora purposely kept the information they'd be meeting his father away from him. That was an issue between Ripper and Demonus, she understood her co-parent and friend's need to disappear.

Ferghus ripped open the gate, metal ground against metal in nails on chalkboard annoyance. "Looking good, the one-armed thing works for ya."

"Bitch," Ferghus grunted.

She only laughed and stepped through it, taking the rank perfume of death. Most there smelled as if decomposition was bone deep.

Amora shoved her hands into her pockets with deceptive calm and followed Kellan. Demonus' quarters were a mile inside the city.

"You're going to explain this if we make it out of here."

"Your Dad needed a safe house, and no one comes to Mael if they don't have any other choice. Just think you're back at the scene of the crime." She lifted her arms and spread them wide. "The place where your parents hatched their plan to fuck Kali over."

"And look at how well that worked for you two," Ripper muttered and fell back.

The rest of the walk was made in silence. She had mixed feelings about seeing her friend again. He'd been there one day and gone the next, no explanations or goodbyes. Again, she understood, he bore the guilt for what awaited their son. Demonus hadn't been ready to submit to Kali's demands and learn to lead in the ways of his father. She had to admit she'd missed her friend, they'd spent more than a century together, fighting back to back, and he'd been the calm to her chaos. The level-head when she killed first and asked questions later.

The lover part of their relationship was brief. Demonus had held copious amounts of hope that she'd come to love him as a mate, but she hadn't been able to change her need for softer flesh over corded muscles. Besides, dick just wasn't her cup of tea, and her acting skills weren't that great. Amora brought her attention back where it should be.

Mael was a strange mix, the edges of the city contained huts and clapboard structures reminiscent of times long past, but toward the center of it were modern buildings. High rises and townhomes, Demonus' house was like one of those scenes where you picked which one didn't belong. It was a bright beacon in a dark landscape. It was elegant and stately, a lot like the demon himself.

She'd never seen her friend mussed, even in battle his hair and bearing made him appear like a king among the ragged and dirty masses. It had a way of pissing her off to no end.

The door opened before they even reached the bottom of the steps and a handsome male stepped out onto the landing. A fallen angel in Armani, he was kind of gorgeous enough to send men and women into a rage of lust. Gods, how she hated him sometimes. "Amora, Rache, are you both insane?"

This wasn't exactly a friendly visit, but at the question, Amora and Ripper started snickering. Insane was in the Medina-Jackyl makeup, or at least it was since she'd become the Matriarch of their little clan of two, now five.

"Hi. Lovely to see you too, Demonus, we missed you."

"Bullshit, my son may have missed me, although he looks as if he would love to remove my head at the moment. Am I safe in assuming you didn't inform him?" The question was rhetorical.

"Dad, nice to see you, been what, fifty-odd years?"

"About that, get your asses inside, I have a reputation to maintain. Associating with the riffraff isn't good for my image."

Amora snickered. "Yeah, yeah."

Kellan stepped to the side. "I'll wait here until you're ready to be led out."

She didn't bother arguing with him to come inside. It was one thing to take a job, but another to consort with the enemy behind closed doors. They feared Demonus for who and what he was, he wore the name Kali like a scarlet K across his chest. She ascended to the landing and entered the open door, Ripper and Demonus brought up the rear.

"Wow, you look like you're doing well for yourself. You taken over this shithole yet?" The place furnished with rich dark woods and warm fabrics. These were not procured in Mael. You were able to get the bare minimums, although with the right price you could get whatever smuggled in.

"No, and I have no intention of doing anything of the sort." His note was disgusted, same old Demonus. If he'd been human, her old friend would've made quite a ruthless businessman, and he already had *the look*. How the fuck had they stayed friends for so long?

The door slammed, and they turned to Ripper. Their reunion wasn't going to be fun. Ripper understood the need to stay under-cover—fly under the proverbial radar. Kali loved to strike out at

Amora, made her life hell, stole her family and freedom, but his most enjoyment came from making Demonus miserable.

"Son, I'm sorry for taking off, but Kali gave me no other choice. I thought Amora would've explained it to you."

"Explained what?" Ripper asked.

"Kali stripped me of my birthright, that you already know, but he officially did it the day I disappeared. I tried to find a loophole, searched high *and* specifically low."

"I get that. I've met the motherfucker, remember? Also, I know what I am, what I have no choice in becoming."

"Again, I'm sorry for not being able to save you from that," Demonus said, his voice filled with regret.

Amora almost took pity on Demonus, but that just wouldn't be her. Like him, she had a reputation to protect, and she was already fighting for it. Too many good deeds and what did they say, good deeds were always punished.

"Either one of you want to tell me what the fuck is going on? Why are we here?"

Finally, down to business and Amora was grateful for the change in subject.

"Kali has been in a bit of a holding pattern for a while now. Locked away like a hermit in his realm. Amora has a feeling Kali freed Boone, and we don't know for what reason."

"Boone is barely a blip on the radar. His reputation as a mass murderer, serial killer and all around exemplary fuck up, but besides that, the vampire has no purpose. Even before he was turned—" Amora paused and strode into the sitting room, she sat on the back of the richly upholstered sofa and crossed her ankles. "He possessed poor impulse control."

"Coming from you that says a lot, Ma."

She only smirked in answer.

Her gaze followed Ripper until he fell back into a chair and motioned for her to continue.

"He has no type, if Boone thinks he can get a hard-on from killing it, then he does it," Amora stated. Boone was proficient in destroying whatever he touched and left whoever behind to remember his work.

Demonus followed and took his seat near a cheerful fire.

"Amora is right for once. I did some checking, and no one trusts him. He's unreliable. When he attacked Ada, his high continues knowing that she'll never forget him or what he did. His fixation, the fact that he's allegedly following her means there's something else at play. Kali isn't even insane enough to employ him."

"But…" Ripper prompted.

Demonus resumed, "Kali's desperate, something isn't right, and I sent a few people to check out the safe house where you found Boone. No scorch marks and they found Selena's ropes severed. This is a witch that kept a demon imprisoned, so she knows what she's doing."

"Lark—" Amora started to speak.

"Lark, who's Lark?"

"Oh, yeah, out of the loop much, ol' man. Ma got herself a sweet little mate."

"Mate?" Demonus turned his attention to her. "You, got a mate, what's wrong with her?"

Ripper burst out with loud guffaws, and Amora turned to glare at him.

"It's not that funny, nothing is wrong with my mate and let's move on. She's not up for discussion."

"Did I forget to mention there's the patter of little feet around the loft too?"

"Oh my Goddess, it's worse than I thought. An impressionable child is involved."

Demonus' statement would almost be laughable if the damn demon wasn't serious about it. Was she that much of a…Amora shook her head, she didn't even have to ask the question. She was a murderous, vengeful fuck up, but Lark was hers, and that's all that mattered.

"Ha, ha, ha, asshole," Amora grumbled.

"Yeah, Lark's only twenty, I asked if she checked I.D."

Ripper wouldn't leave her mate's age alone. One more comment about jailbait and she'd kill him just for the fun of it, son or not. Okay, she couldn't kill him, but she could make him suffer plenty.

"I will kill you both, and here, I'd get away with it. The bodies wouldn't even have to be hidden. Back to Boone and Kali's motive."

"Kali doesn't need a reason, he has hatred, specifically hatred for you," Demonus stated.

"There's has to be something about Ada or her past. Lark thinks he's using Ada to draw us out—start a war." Amora was growing tired of Kali's hard-on for her. Before Lark and Ada, she'd handled it with a sense of twisted amusement. Making Kali's life difficult was simply her way of passing her existence. There had to be something more— what that more was pushed her toward madness. She needed the answers. Amora's limited loyalties were expanding. She had people other than Ripper now, three innocent lives to protect—family.

"Now the war I could agree with. Kali loves to make our lives as impossible as he can. There's nothing remotely remarkable about Ada's past. One of six children, single mother, allegations of abuse, sexual and otherwise, by her mother's many boyfriends." Demonus pushed his fingers through his thick blond hair. "She showed up at Herder's not long after she turned eighteen. She's been there ever since. One of his most popular, until Boone turned up."

"Same thing I came up with. Boone doesn't serve a purpose, but I'm positive Ada does."

"You showed her kindness, Amora, maybe Kali looked at her like a weak link for you. It could just be coincidence," Demonus suggested.

"To think The Great Amora Medina-Jackyl has a weak link, Kali would have gotten a hard-on just at the thought of it."

"Kali and hard-on in the same sentence, don't ever do that again." It wasn't as if she hadn't thought of it herself, he wouldn't let it go. And until he was banished or dead, she and her family would never live in peace. That wasn't something she wanted to deal with right then. First, they had to get through this battle, the war could wait.

They settled in to brainstorm, and unfortunately, by the end, Amora knew they wouldn't be closer to the answers they needed.

CHAPTER 26

*I*t was early, the sun hadn't even started to rise outside their tent and Lark didn't hear movement outside. Lark quickly realized she couldn't sleep without Amora. Knowing her mate was off somewhere defending them and making sure the family they were creating was safe, put her on edge. She couldn't deny her mate her obsession. It was odd really, the way her life had changed in such a short time.

Was it possible mere months ago she'd resigned herself to life in The Order and her fate to being the vessel for future killers? The memories of Reginald's threats of what he had planned for her caused her to shiver in fear. Her life wasn't any safer now, although she felt secure as Amora's mate.

She cast a glance toward Meadow and Ada sleeping on pallets near the wall of their temporary home. A smile tugged at the corners of her mouth then her happy expression fell. How was she—a mere mortal— supposed to keep them safe? She wasn't Amora or Ripper. She didn't possess the killer instinct, no matter the hardships or the horrors she faced, she was still the disappointing pacifist her parents hated.

Lark still didn't understand her place at Amora's side. She knew she could comfort her mate and bring her peace when the battles took her to the edge of whatever sanity Amora had left. Yet could she fight beside Amora, draw blood in combat? Lark knew she couldn't. She would do what she was able, beyond that...only time would tell.

An explosion rocked the ground beneath her bare feet. She froze as terror turned her vision blurry, and she swayed on her feet.

"Lark!" Meadow's cry pushed her into action.

She ran to her sister and scooped the child into her arms. Holding her one-armed as little arms and legs wrapped tightly around her. Lark grabbed Ada's slender hand and pulled her up. "We have to get to safety," she whispered.

The sounds of battle outside, screams, hisses and great roars. Beast and man fought, smoke filled the interior of the tent and all three coughed. Lark noticed Ada held tight to the knife Amora had given her before she and Ripper had left, Lark's own strapped in a slim holster at the small of her back. Her mate made her promise never to be without it, and she'd elicited the same vow from Ada.

They scurried toward the rear exit that Amora had made with a slit in the tent for their escape. She knew where to go, there was a small cave system a mile from camp. If anything was to happen, they were to hide there until Amora came for them. "Grab the pack," she told Ada. The Go-Bag as Amora called it contained food, bottled water and other essentials—at least a few days' worth.

She watched as Ada shouldered the back, nearly stumbling under the weight—proof that Ada wasn't a hundred percent.

They didn't have much time, she knew it was The Order, and they'd attacked too close to sunrise to lessen Seamus' vampire numbers. Although they had an hour until sunrise, The Order may have jumped the gun a bit. She had hope that the vampires survived.

"We're going where Amora told us to go. You'll hold onto me, no matter what, promise me, Ada."

The only answer she received was a nod, wide, terrified eyes met hers, and she turned away to hide her own. She had one job—Amora trusted her—Lark could do this. Lark wrapped herself around Meadow trying to obscure the stark white of Amora's shirt Meadow wore.

Cool, early morning air surrounded them as they exited and they started running. She heard shouts behind them, but she didn't stop she see if anyone followed. Amora had shown Lark the best places to evade, a small copse of tightly grouped trees larger men wouldn't find easy to enter. It was only a mile away, heavy steps pounded the ground and debris crunched under bulky boots, but she ignored it.

It was still dark, but Amora had taken her along the escape route, and Lark's photographic memory worked in her favor. Meadow trembled against her chest. She paused to get her bearings and check if the bastards were still following them.

"Come out, come out, wherever you are." A sinister singsong voice caused Ada to push to her back.

"It's him, we have—" Ada gasped and then went silent.

"Did you think Amora would do away with me? That you'd survive," Boone taunted them. "Come out, bitch, you screamed so prettily when I stripped the flesh from your body. I want to see that beautiful smile I gave you."

Ada's heavy breathing turned to panting gasps, Lark could feel the other woman ready to have a panic attack.

"Amora isn't here. The ones she left to protect you failed. I promise after a few screams, I'll take you quickly before I slit your throat. Only a small suffering, I owe that to you after the beautiful symphony of your screams the last time."

Lark felt the need to puke burn at the back of her throat. Ada's scars told enough of the story, of the torture and pain, but to hear it and know what the bastard did was too much. Ada trembled uncontrollably beside her. Seemingly ready to break.

"Don't make me find you, I'll make it even worse for you," Boone promised.

Lark realized the direction of where his voice came from changed, growing louder and as she focused, she could hear the shifting of his feet as he drew nearer.

"Amora can't save you, it was your worst mistake when you sent that vamp after me."

They couldn't stay there, he'd find them, but his voice was too close. From her experience with Amora, she knew how quickly a vampire would overtake them. She slipped one arm from around Meadow and reached back to take Ada's hand. They'd move slow and steady. Low hanging branches snagged on their clothes, scraped along the exposed skin. The stinging abrasions barely registered as they moved and listened to Boone. It was a constant barrage of innuendo and threats. He replayed everything he'd done to the woman, and Ada grew stiffer behind her. Ada held herself so tightly, Lark swore she'd crumble at any moment.

"He doesn't matter, you're safe, you're our family and Amora won't let anything happen to us." Lark spun, and Ada's ashen face nearly glowed in the darkness. "Tell me you understand, we belong to Amora Jackyl, a warrior-borne, she'll fight through Hell and back for us. We're her family, her anchor, Ada, tell me you understand?" she demanded in a quiet, yet fierce tone.

"I understand," Ada agreed.

Lark didn't believe it though, Ada hadn't had many promises of good—of family in her life, but she'd make sure the girl always knew that she belonged with them.

"We may not be Jackyl's by birth, but it's our family, and we fight for our own." Tears burned her eyes, but she refused to let them fall. Later when she's in bed, secure in her mate's arms, she'd let herself fall apart.

"Momma's coming." Meadow's words were muffled against Lark's chest.

She looked down to find her baby sister innocently smiling up at her. She wondered what damage the first four years of belonging to The Order caused to Meadow, what struggles awaited them. Meadow was always different, serenity in her bearing even through hell, the little girl stayed quiet—introspective. Lark wanted more for Meadow, a happy childhood and a loving family. Being with Amora wouldn't make that easy, but Lark wouldn't have it any other way.

"Close your eyes, Meadow."

"I know." The little girl squeezed her eyes shut. "Momma said so."

Confused, but unable to question Meadow, she held still and looked directly into Ada's gaze.

"Come out, bitches, I don't have all night." Boone's voice steadily grew from calm to maniacal, pitching octaves higher.

A scream ripped through the darkness, then another, and another. Smoke filled the air as the breeze turned and the battle seemed to have come to them.

"Kali must've been high when he thought you'd be helpful." Amora amused voice made Lark smile, and Meadow giggled. "Oh, that's right, Kali owns what's left of your soul. Mael not exactly the vacation destination of your choice?"

"Give her to me, Jackyl, I'll let you have the other two. That mate of yours is a little too big for my tastes, but that kid—" Boone made a humming sound. "Maybe when she's older."

An enraged hiss broke through Lark's horror at the threat to Meadow.

With unspoken intent, the three of them moved closer to the edge of the trees until the faint glow of the rising sun tinted the sky. Beasts and humans alike surrounded Boone and Amora, a circle of protection. Her mate circled Boone, her eyes black and her fangs distended.

"Lark, come on." Ripper's voice pulled her attention away from what she could see of her mate. "Amora needs you three."

She didn't understand why the most dominant killer in history would need her, but she didn't question it. Lark sank into the comfort of her stepson's arm around her shoulders. She quickly found herself on Seamus' left, the line of bodies moving to allow room for Amora's family. Seamus began to speak.

"We've done battle countless times, we've stood together as a pack of outcasts, and today once more we've come out the victors. Our pack law allows for retribution. An outsider has attacked our family, Amora may challenge to the death the ones responsible. What say you, Amora, death or banishment?"

"Ada," Amora whispered.

The tenderness in that tone no longer shocked Lark.

Lark observed Amora approach, her long, lean body covered in blood and new wounds. She wanted to go to her mate, but something was coming, and she needed to wait. Amora stood before them.

"Under Seamus' law, I may accept anyone into my family. An adoption of sorts and I know Lark has already said you'll come to live with us. You're family, and I protect those who are mine. You haven't been given much in the way of power, so I'll ask this as my daughter, his fate is yours, what do you want? Death or his return below?"

Lark turned her head to find tears streaming down Ada's pale cheeks. Lark never thought it would happen, she was even more in awe of her mate. Amora knew what Ada needed—closure—to stop looking over her shoulder again. The road ahead for Ada was still long and being a Jackyl by birth, or by choice wasn't the easiest life to live.

"Death," Ada stated emphatically.

"Very well. Boone, hand to hand combat or weapons, it's your only choice." She looked up to find Amora watching her. A loving glow in her onyx eyes and Lark smiled at her mate.

"You can't let that thing have the choice, she's nothing, a piece of ass—a meal. Nothing more!" Boone's voice was hysterical.

"You're just digging yourself deeper, fucker, and I'm going to enjoy this one."

The warmth that existed moments before disappeared as the monster took over. She'd known before, but to see her mate readying for battle was different. This was a warrior going to war for their Clan, and Lark squared her shoulders, held her head high. Amora fought for them, the ones she loved, and she would make her mate proud.

Amora pivoted, the twin blades slid with a whisper of sound from the sheaths at her back.

"Send me back, I'll go—" The words were cut off by the arc of Amora's arm. Blood fell in a crimson rain as Amora attacked. There was a surreal beauty in it, the dance of a warrior's skill honed over time in choreographed perfection. It was almost too easy, Boone fought, but Amora outmatched him. Even the knife that somehow made it into Boone's hand didn't increase his odds of survival.

Boone got lucky, striking out wildly and drawing minimal blood.

Ada gasped, Meadow kept her face tucked into Lark's neck and still it continued. It was as if the world ceased to exist, no one on the battlefield except a soldier hardened by battle scars and horrors.

Screams rang out, pleas for mercy and the blissed-out expression on her mate's face didn't change. Lark should be frightened of the coldness—the abject joy Amora took in the wounds and damage she inflicted, but Amora did that for them.

The crowd that was once silent rang out in cheers as Boone fell to his knees before Amora. The sun cresting the horizon, smoke filling the air as flesh began to burn and turn to ash. When she expected to see the final wound, a slit throat or a broken neck, they didn't come. Ripper rushed in, wrapped a thick black tapestry around Amora and led her from the circle.

"Can you stay with me?" Ada asked.

"Of course." Lark twined one arm around her adopted daughter and held Meadow tighter with the other.

Ada needed to see, as much as it sickened Lark to watch something that could easily happen to Amora, she couldn't leave.

Sparks flew as flesh ignited. Skin, muscle and sinew turned to black, exposed the bone below. And the smell of it was nauseating in its sickening sweet smell. At the edges, she realized the crowd dispersed.

"Amora will be waiting, take your time. She'll understand. This is your place, Lark, you have the most daunting job of all. You're their peace, their rock when they think they can no longer go on. I pity and envy you your love."

She only nodded at Seamus' words and brought her attention back to Ada.

"Should I feel something? I sentenced him to death, made Amora kill him."

"You feel what you want to feel, retribution was yours, Ada, and Amora won't blame you. She understands vengeance more than any of us ever will, the need to be free. Come, let's go home, get you bathed. Your life is your own now, the power is yours, but use Amora's gift well."

"I promise," Ada said.

It was all Lark could ask as Ada turned away and preceded her. "Meadow," she whispered her sister's name.

"I love you, Mama Lark," Meadow said and looked up at her.

Lark didn't realize she was crying until tiny, chunky hands wiped the tears from her face. So little time had passed, and everything was different—would always be that way. There was no doubt in Lark, she was exactly where she needed to be and where she was destined to stay.

"I love you too, baby girl, let's go home to Momma 'Mora."

Lark turned and made her way through the trees, the morning sun and breeze was warm as the chill of night receded. The fear and stress of the previous hour caused her body to become cumbersome. All she wanted was to go home to Amora—their family—and sleep in her mate's arms. She replayed Seamus' words in her head, she, Lark the pacifist, was the foundation of a family of warriors. She was their comfort when their strength momentarily broke, and tears fell.

It was a daunting task, but she couldn't deny it. This was her fate, what she'd been born to do and be, and she'd never take it lightly. She was a Medina-Jackyl by choice, and as she'd told Ada, theirs wouldn't be the easy life to live, although she'd have it no other way.

EPILOGUE

*S*haggy blond hair fell to conceal her son's unusual green eyes, the bright yellow flare of color around the slight, slender, vertical pupil. She studied him as she had many times before, a human wouldn't notice the slight deformity, yet other preternatural species would. It was the mark of his curse—the prophesized Hell he lived with. Amora Medina-Jackyl didn't know what to do with her son, hell, she didn't even know where to fucking start. It was simply there, brought about by her and his father's need to disgrace the Soul Collector Demon Kali, her son's grandfather.

In the centuries since she'd went to battle once more with Kali, she'd found a semblance of peace. The new comfort of her mate, it was like decaying dreams slowing blossoming back to life. Part of her still existed for the vengeance and blood, the pain. To avenge her family who Kali and The Order of Angelus took from her still filled her with bloodlust.

Ripper gazed out into the coming dawn. Fuck, she was such a bitch she even named her son the German word for revenge. The demon/vampire hybrid Amora watched had grown into a weary male, and it was her fault. Amora had plenty of regrets and what she'd turned him into may be her greatest one—not even the countless lives she'd taken in her over four centuries reached the level of the curse she'd placed on her son's head the moment of his conception.

"Regrets don't look good on you," Ripper softly whispered.

She knew he kept his voice quiet as not to disturb her mate and her young sister. "Who the fuck said I was regretting anything?"

"Hell, we've fought back to back since I was old enough to wield a blade. I think I need some time—to think."

"You mean time to run. Your fate was sealed the moment I fucked —" Ripper's gag cut her off and she had to grin.

"Please, I don't need a blow by blow of your coital escapades with your co-parent and best friend."

"Lark's my best friend, your sperm donor comes in maybe second, or third."

"You're such a bitch." Ripper smiled as he said it.

"That's not news. Where will you go?"

"I just need time."

"What about her?"

"Who?"

"You know who the fuck we're talking about. It's time, Rache, to claim your happiness."

"Don't call me that. Could you have picked a worse name?"

"Probably, now, quit changing the subject, answer me," Amora demanded. She lounged with a deceptive ease in her favorite chair and studied the half-completed canvas of Lark. Her innocent mate nearly died from embarrassment finding Amora painting her nude, but the woman's curves drove her insane.

"I can't claim her, Ma. What do I have to offer her, but a life wasted with me. I'm nothing more than a parasite or will be."

"There's more to being a Soul Collector than feeding off others, you're more stubborn than I am. I've told you countless times to contact Demonus. It's well past time for it to happen and have that talk about your future."

She didn't flinch when her beautiful son turned on her with rage burning in his gaze. The ripple of onyx scales traversing his tanned skin in agitation, yet he didn't let the anger force his change into his demon form of a serpent.

"My whole fucking life is a guillotine blade ready to fall, the choices aren't simple." He swung his arms wide and began to pace. "Either I embrace my fate as the next in line for Kali's twisted throne and kill the old bastard or try to live with as much normalcy as I can. The latter gets me the exact thing I crave, she's all I want or think about. How can I sentence her to the Hell that is an eternity with me, tell me, Ma?"

"I can't tell you. What if your mate—the one you deny—can give you what Lark gave me? We protect what and who are ours, it's the one right thing I taught you. But you're foolish to deny the one person who could make you and your demon coexist."

"There's no coexisting; we're one and the same. He's tearing me apart more and more each day. Her scent still lingers downstairs, it's as if claws are ripping at my gut. I just need time, please, give me that, and I'll begin my search for Nicolette."

The pleading in Ripper's voice caressed over what little humanity she possessed, even as the name of her sister broke a piece of her blackened heart. She still saw Nicolette's face in her nightmares, the trusting, beautiful visage, and she'd failed the young vampire just as she'd let down the rest of her siblings. The flames glowed in the hazy windows locked in frames of stone, their cries as they burned and she was useless to help. Child or not, her parents taught her to fight, to protect—family above all else. Nico hopefully lived, at least one survived her mistakes and weaknesses.

"You have your time, Ripper. Centuries have passed, a little longer doesn't matter, but your mate and demon won't wait. Be quick in your soul searching. Believe me when I tell you chances at happiness are fleeting, don't waste yours over some false sense of pride and protectiveness." Before she watched the hazy dematerialization of Ripper's form, he gave her a small nod and disappeared. She didn't bother asking where he was headed. If anything, her son was exactly like her, stubborn and secretive. Amora would let him have his time—for now.

* * *

THE TABLE SET with glittering crystal carafes that held blood and platters of food for Ripper and the humans of her family covered the entire surface. It turned out Ada cooked when she was nervous, happy or bored. Amora saw so much food. It was a good thing she was well off, or her daughter would break her.

She cast her gaze around the table. Lark was to her right, Ripper her left, and Ada and Meadow beside them. There were still empty places at the table she swore she'd fill one of these days, no matter if it took years or centuries she'd find them.

In some part of her mind, memories she'd fought hard to keep at bay came back full force. Meals with her parents and siblings, laughter and love—it was strange to think she could have something like that again. Amora remembered being happy, even if they spent their time on high alert and ready for any battle. Could she do that now with Lark—make her feel as if the struggle was worth it. All the absences and death were part of being her mate, but would Lark grow tired of waiting—of loving the deadly creature Amora was?

Maybe after, when all this ended, and her family was home—when she no longer had to fight—she'd make it up to her innocent Lark. She wasn't able to give up the small sliver of hope her failure hadn't lost Amora her siblings. Amora needed patience and time, neither of which she possessed much of.

"What's wrong, love?" Lark asked, her small hand covering Amora's.

"Nothing, I just wish—" She couldn't continue. Expressing her wishes never succeeded in getting her anywhere.

"We'll find them, even if it's just to give them a proper goodbye. Nicolette was alive until a century ago, after that she disappeared. Medina-Jackyl's don't lay down and die. She's alive, and we'll have her home soon."

Lark's faith eased her tensed muscles. It still amazed her after nearly half a year that this was now her life, no longer an existence to be suffered. Time measured in body count or another bounty, or random warm bodies to make her feel even for a brief time.

Ripper looked over at her. "I have a few leads to follow up on Lark gave me, I'll be headed out in the morning."

She'd expected it and would let it go, no fight would keep him there. "You've stayed longer than I expected you too."

"It's too much to stay," Ripper admitted.

She knew her son fought his demon for what it desired and to be so close to his mate and not to claim tore him apart. Kali would fall, Rache would ascend, and she'd lose the son she'd raised. The vampire —the Medina-Jackyl—would almost cease to exist and he would be what he was destined to be. The Soul Collector.

THE END

ABOUT THE AUTHOR

J.M. Dabney is a multi-genre author who writes mainly LGBT romance and fiction. She lives with a constant diverse cast of characters in her head. No matter their size, shape, race, etc. she lives for one purpose alone, and that's to make sure she does them justice and give them the happily ever after they deserve. J.M. is dysfunction at its finest and she makes sure her characters are a beautiful kaleidoscope of crazy. There is nothing more she wants from telling her stories than to show that no matter the package the characters come in or the damage their pasts have done, that love is love. That normal is never normal and sometimes the so-called broken can still be amazing.